I0622113

UNDERGROUND SOCIETY: VOLUME 1-2 - THE DUEL COLLECTION

DOMINIC R. DANIELS
&
RAYNALDO D. DELEON II

Dedicated to Phil & Mary Daniels

WGA REGISTERED

DOMINIC ROCKY DANIELS
Email: dominicdaniels777@gmail.com

Raynaldo D. Deleon II
Email: therondeleon@gmail.com

FADE IN:

EXT. CALIFORNIA ROAD - EARLY MORNING
Enter KEN LIU, 30s, a young and tough Chinese man. Dressed in slick black suit and dress shoes and dark sunglasses, he carries a black briefcase and gun.

Ken is bloody and bruised. This guy's been through some heavy action. But he remains calm. And his manner and voice are those of a deep thinker.

                         KEN (V.O.)
          I never realized, how one mistake a man could make...
          could change the course of his whole life.

Ken walks down the open highway. He lights a cigarette with a vintage Zippo.

Ken reaches a bus stop and sits down on the bench. Smokes. The cleansing tar and nicotine seem to ease his mind.

                         KEN (V.O.) (CONT'D)
          My name is Ken Liu. Well... that's one of my names. A
          professional assassin for the Chinese Triad. Killing is the
          business I'm in. Once, it was the last thing I would've
          done. But eventually, you get so you enjoy it. When that
          happens, you know you're damned for all eternity.
                              (beat)

But I guess... it was in my blood...

FLASHBACK - EXT. CHINATOWN (SAN FRANCISCO) - DAY

SUPER: "SAN FRANCISCO, 1985"

San Francisco's Chinatown -- curio shops, people selling their exotic wares. The smoke of ethnic cooking from noodle shops and Chinese BBQ restaurants hangs in the air.

In a little shop, Ken's mother JUNE FEI, 40s, lifts her five-year-old son KEN. She hugs the child, then puts him down. Nearby, her older son SAM FEI, (10) and daughter, ANN FEI (8) run and play.

Nearby, WONG CHOU FEI, 40s, a tough, experience-scarred man, smiles happily down on them.

> KEN (V.O.)
>
> My given name was Ken Chou Fei. My parents did
> their best to insulate me from my family's past. But
> Hong Kong has a way of following you everywhere...

FLASHBACK - INT. CRIME FAMILY MANSION (HONG KONG) - NIGHT

SUPER: "HONG KONG, 1980"

Wong, with a moustache and short goatee, wearing a slick black suit, creeps forward -- and slowly pulls out twin pistols with silencers.

> KEN (V.O.)
>
> The way of the gun... you live by it and you die by it.

Wong moves through the house, shooting his two pistols in surgical bursts. Gangster after gangster falls to this black-suited ghost.

> KEN (V.O.) (CONT'D)
>
> Like the angel of death, my father came quickly and struck.
> His reason -- honor among Tong. Loyal to his family.

Wong steps lightly over the threshold and into the night. Behind him, carnage and drifting smoke. Not a thing lives.

INT. WHITE LOTUS LOUNGE BANQUET ROOM - NIGHT
Wong is feted by a group of men at a long table, covered with an array of dishes and traditional Asian delights. And some other Asian delights -- high class call girls.

Suddenly police sweep in. The gang members are taken into custody. The cops nod at Wong. He's not cuffed.

> KEN (V.O.)
> To redeem himself, my father did the last thing any Tong
> would ever dare. He betrayed them. He was a cop.

SERIES OF SHOTS
In the office of a large warehouse, Wong and Ken's grandfather LIU CHOW FEI, 60s, crouch furtively by a large safe.

> KEN (V.O.)
> But not all the way straight...

Liu flicks the combination with an expert hand. Opens the safe on stacks of Chinese yuan --

> KEN (V.O.) (CONT'D)
> He was desperate to give my family and me a better
> life. A price that would be paid in blood.

Lights go on. Tong appear, take hold of the men. Some of them we saw in the previous scene. They don't look happy.

Wong and Liu attack their captors, and escape from custody. A running battle ensues in the warehouse. Liu is shot, falls back in Wong's arms.

KEN (V.O.) (CONT'D)
My father promised my grandfather he'd take care of
the family...

Liu dies. Wong, enraged, operates his machine gun like a conductor's baton --
everywhere it points, death follows.

Wong escapes from the warehouse and hops into his car. He speeds off into
the night.

KEN (V.O.) (CONT'D)
My mother, a police secretary, loved him for his integrity. Ironic. He spent so much of his life in deep cover...

Wong and June, and the children, smaller, teeter on a crappy ferry steaming away
from the city.

KEN (V.O.) (CONT'D)
...A fate he passed on to his family. We spent our whole
lives in hiding.

June chucks baby Ken under the chin.

KEN (V.O.) (CONT'D)
I was just a baby. What the hell did I know? To me, this
life was normal.

Wong kisses his baby and his wife.

KEN (V.O.) (CONT'D)
They raised me well. They wanted something better for their kids. We had a good home, but it wasn't
meant to be. Hong Kong... has a way of following you.
Everywhere.

FLASHBACK - EXT. CHINATOWN - FEIS' MARKET - DAY

SUPER: "SAN FRANCISCO, 2000's"
Ken, now 30s, bright and sharp as a tack, heads down the alley of shops toward his parents' stall.

> KEN (V.O.)
> I'd just graduated from Harvard Business School, and I came home to reunite with my family. I was hoping to get a job close to home, maybe start a little business of my own in time.

As Ken meets with his father in front of the shop, there is a black car parked on a curb with some gangsters inside. One older man, from the back seat, sees Wong and does a double-take. He dials his cell phone as the car drives off.

SERIES OF SHOTS
In a comfortable home, Wong and June bustle about preparing dishes and laying a table in grand Asian fashion. Sam and Ann help. They are laughing and merry. Then they look up. Masked gunmen appear in the entry hall, one by one. They brandish Uzis. A firing squad.

> KEN (V.O.)
> In the end, the Tongs came back...

The gunmen open fire. The meal is shot to hell, along with the four family members. Noodles, dumplings and rice -- blood and bullets.

One gunman notices a small tai-chi amulet. He smiles through his mask. And pockets it.

Ken arrives outside and looks up to see the masked gunmen, guns smoking, jump into cars and speed off.

His face terrorized, he runs into the house.

> KEN (V.O.) (CONT'D)
> I tried to save them, but it was too late...

The house looks quiet, from outside. But from inside:

> KEN (CONT'D)
>
> Noooo!!

Later, their mangled faces are zipped into body bags. The bodies are wheeled past Ken into a pair of ambulances.

> KEN (V.O.) (CONT'D)
> The past was stronger than I was. It would destroy everything in its path. That's how the spirit of death works. If follows you like cockroaches and never lets go.

The ambulances drive off, without lights or siren.

Locals -- hardworking older couples and the odd youngster -- stare on, crying and shocked.

Ken stares, face cold.

INT. GAS STATION BATHROOM - MORNING (BACK TO PRESENT)

That coldness remains in his face. In a dingy, scummy bathroom, Ken stands with his shirt off. His chest and arms are crisscrossed with bruises and wounds.

He opens a suitcase. Two pristine Desert Eagle pistols sit, atop a great deal of cash. He roots around in there for a small bottle of alcohol.

> KEN (V.O.)
> That's right. I'm a professional killer, an assassin for hire. The Los Angeles Triads, Zao Sun's division.

He disinfects his wounds. Grits his teeth at the pain.

                    KEN (V.O.) (CONT'D)
How'd I wind up in this position? Funny thing.

Ken looks deeply into his own face in the mirror. His expression impassive.

                    KEN (V.O.) (CONT'D)
The more you try and fight your fate... the deeper its
hold on you. When you take life, in this life or the last,
your soul is cursed forever.

FLASHBACK - INT. SAN FRANCISCO - FUNERAL - DAY
Ken stands, expressionless, in a dark suit at a funeral. His aunt MEI MING and
uncle WEN MING, 40s, flank him. On the other side, cousin HUNG MING, 30s.

                      KEN (V.O.)
All that I had in life had been taken. So I had nothing
left to lose. All I knew was... I wanted some payback.
Justice really.

INT. NIGHT OWL BAR - NIGHT
A small but chill bar and lounge. The club is playing slow jazz music.
     MIKE LEE, 30s, young, flashy, dressed like the hotshot lawyer he is, lifts a
glass next to Ken at the bar. The boys clink and drink.

                        KEN
Thanks for helping me out, Mike.

                        MIKE
I'm sorry for your loss. I know it's rough for you.

                        KEN
I wish I could get the bastards who killed my family.

MIKE

What's stopping you?

KEN

The culture. I reported the Tongs to the police. They just laughed. One of the cops took me aside and said: "Mr. Fei, you don't want to report them anyway. They'll find you and kill you. Let it go."

He takes another slug.

KEN (CONT'D)

I'm not letting this go. I should be out there getting payback. It's bullshit. What the hell is the point of justice if the cops and courts won't help you get it?

Ken upends his glass, signals for another. Mike gets an idea.

MIKE

Say, listen. I know a guy. A very powerful man. He has some pretty heavy connections... he might be able to help in this situation.

KEN

I'm listening.

MIKE

If I contact him, he'll want a favor from you...and it won't be cheap.

KEN

I don't care. I got nothing to lose. So what does it matter?

INT. FEI HOUSE - AFTERNOON

Ken walks around the Fei house. All the gore is gone -- everything is gone. The house is empty, like Ken's life.

A knock on the door. Ken answers. Mike enters, with MR. ZAO SUN, 60s -- hard as a rock, but with a certain kindness in his eyes.

> KEN
>
> Glad you stopped by, Mike.

> MIKE
>
> Ken Fei -- this is Mr. Zao Sun.

> MR. SUN
>
> My condolences on your loss. I know how hard it is to have your loved ones taken from you. I was dear friends with your father a long time ago, we were colleagues at one time.

> KEN
>
> Thank you.

> MIKE
>
> I've asked Mr. Sun if he can offer you a position in one of his enterprises.

> MR. SUN
>
> Michael tells me you graduated top of your class at Harvard. Tell me, what are your future plans?

> KEN
>
> Get a job here in the Bay area, if possible.

> MR. SUN
>
> Why don't you relocate?

                    KEN
This is my home. Why should I?

                  MR. SUN
The Tongs, son, that's why. The Tongs will come after
you next. Once they start a job to kill someone they
don't stop and they will kill you if you stay.

                  MR. SUN
I'm only saying this because I respected your father and
I would hate to see his only surviving son get killed.
You have many impressive skills, I can put that to good
use for you, if you'll let me.

Ken hadn't considered that.

              MR. SUN (CONT'D)
Listen, to me Ken. I own a prestigious art gallery in
Beverly Hills. It is in need of a new manager to run the
place.

                    KEN
What happen to the old manager?

Mr. Sun smiles faintly.

                  MR. SUN
Let's just say he's currently pursuing a new career
track... elsewhere.

                    MIKE
The pay's excellent and the job comes with plenty of
great perks. As your lawyer, and friend, Ken, I advise

you to take it. Besides, LA is filled to the brim with privileges, you will like it, trust me.

Ken turns to the room where his parents and siblings died. He walks, silently, thinking.

> KEN (V.O.)
> I was reluctant. What the did I know about art? But Mike was being transferred to L.A. -- and his connections were worth their weight in gold...

Mike and Mr. Sun wait in respectful silence.
Ken comes to the wall. It's pocked with bullet holes. He stares at them.

> KEN (V.O.) (CONT'D)
> I'd be a fool to turn it down. Even if the country wasn't going down the toilet economically. So I took the job.

Ken returns to the men, decision made.

> KEN (CONT'D)
> Thank you, Mr. Sun. I appreciate this opportunity.

Ken shakes Mr. Sun's hand. Mr. Sun smiles. There's power and danger in that smile.

EXT. FEI HOUSE - MOMENTS LATER
Mike and Mr. Sun return to a black limousine parked out front.

> MIKE
> Should we tell him about finding the Tongs?

MR. SUN

He doesn't need to know.

EXT. TONG HIDEOUT - NIGHT

A group of men hang out in a richly appointed living room. Guns, drugs and money are all in evidence.

One of the men, with a familiar smile, dangles the tai-chi amulet he took from the Fei house. He laughs, and puts the amulet on over his neck.

KEN (V.O.)

Mr. Sun did take care of things...

Triad members appear from doors and windows like magic. The Tong gang members freeze, one sudden moment of surprise.

And the gunfire starts. All are slain.

The tai-chi is shot through the center. Its wearer spits up blood.

KEN (V.O.) (CONT'D)

And like Mike said... once Mr. Sun does you a favor, you owe him a favor. And he would certainly collect.

EXT. BEVERLY HILTON HOTEL - NIGHT

SUPER: "Los Angeles"

A white limo arrives. Mr. Sun and his entourage -- including Ken -- get out of the limo.

KEN (V.O.)

Within a matter of months, I've been making bank as an art dealer and manager. I had a new name, to keep the Tongs off my ass -- Ken Liu. That new name felt like a new life. I had it all.

> KEN (V.O.)
>
> Posh cars, flashy suits, jewels, and piles of enough cash
> so thick that it could be a mattress made of money fit
> for a king to sleep on. Well that was not all; there was
> also the girl of my dreams, Maggie.

MAGGIE SUN, late 20s, sweet and innocent, is at Ken's side.

> KEN (V.O.) (CONT'D)
>
> The prettiest girl in town -- Mr. Sun's daughter, Maggie.
> An angel, fresh from heaven that flew down and land-
> ed right into my lap. She was the best.

INT. BEVERLY HILTON HOTEL - WILSHIRE BALLROOM - NIGHT
Inside the ballroom, everyone sits at dinner tables, eating, drinking and smoking. A jazz band blazes on the stage.

> KEN (V.O.)
>
> I was rolling with the in crowd, visiting the trendiest
> places and parties. It was a pleasure.

Ken and Mr. Sun sit at a large table with other associates.
    Ken Liu, Mr. Sun and his entourage meet with other Sun Members.

> KEN (V.O.) (CONT'D)
>
> I was accepted into the inner circle. That's Mr. Sun's
> entourage of trusted associates.

JOHNNY WU, 30s, laughs at something.

> KEN (V.O.) (CONT'D)
>
> That's Johnny Wu, vice president of the business. Mr.
> Sun's lieutenant. A loyal man and role model for the
> rest us.

Johnny's laughing at some clowning from ZAN and TAI, 20s.

> KEN (V.O.) (CONT'D)
> Those two guys, that's Zan & Tai, childhood friends
> and class clowns... that is, at least if they would've been
> had they ever gone to school.

BENNY WONG, 20s, laughs along, on the fringes.

> KEN (V.O.) (CONT'D)
> And Benny Wong, the new guy. Young but smart.

Suddenly a new group arrives -- the Malone family.

> KEN (V.O.) (CONT'D)
> Mr. Sun was meeting business partners and associates
> -- the Malone family, that night.

DON GINO, 60s, shakes Mr. Sun's hand warmly. He's flanked by his nephew
PAUL, late 30s, and Gino's brother. CARMINE, 50s.

> KEN (V.O.) (CONT'D)
> Angelo LaMotta Malone, Jr. -- better known as Gino.
> He was the head president of one of the largest cor-
> porate banks in the states and a wealthy entrepreneur
> throughout L.A. county. That's his brother, Carmine
> with him.

Behind Don Gino, bearing a family resemblance, JIMMY, 30s, and TOMMY,
20s.

> KEN (V.O.) (CONT'D)
> And his boys, Jimmy and Tommy. Jimmy was mature
> for his age. Dependable. Tommy, on the other hand...

little prick. The brat of the family. Always a hot head and hard ass to deal with.

Tommy sneers at the others, stares at the ass of a passing female.

INT. BEVERLY HILTON HOTEL - WILSHIRE BALLROOM - LATER
The mood seems congenial. Except for Tommy, who calls out, laughs loudly, and swills champagne.
Ken leans over to Jimmy and speaks quietly under the noise of the band.

> KEN
> (glances at Tommy)

He okay?

> JIMMY

Yeah, yeah. He's a little shit, whaddaya gonna do. My name's Jimmy.

> KEN

Ken... Ken Liu.

> JIMMY

You new around here?

> KEN

Yeah, from San Francisco. How 'bout you?

> JIMMY

Miami, Florida.

> KEN

So what do you do?

JIMMY

I work in construction management and real estate. I buy, sell and flip houses. Anyway, I heard you're pretty smart guy.

KEN

I heard the same about you.

JIMMY

You blowin' smoke up my ass?

KEN

Never on a first date.

The both crack up.

KEN (V.O.) (CONT'D)

Me and Jimmy became friends faster than a quarter mile race. Charismatic as hell. He also introduced me to some of his extended family and oh boy was it huge.

Jimmy shows Ken around the ballroom, getting him to shake hands with other people around the place. They all come from various other nationalities. Ken shakes hands with gentlemen who are Mexican, Russian, Israeli and others.

KEN (V.O.) (CONT'D)

Amazing how someone could have such a diverse family. Jimmy was a really great guy, but there was only one person who stayed on my mind, most of the time.

INT. BEVERLY HILTON HOTEL - WILSHIRE BALLROOM - LATER
Ken dances with Maggie. Tommy watches. He's drunker now.

KEN (V.O.)

I was so over the moon for Maggie. I'd do anything for her... even die, if necessary. She meant the world to me.

Tommy has an eye for Maggie. He leaves to get a cigarette.

Meanwhile, the heads of the two families are deep in conversation.

DON GINO

We got your shipments from China and our partners from Colombia are sending theirs.

MR. SUN

I'm glad to hear that.

PAUL

The word is that the Bazins' corporation is trying to legally take over.

CARMINE

Those Arab pricks. Who do they think they are? They got nothing but bullshit. Fuck them.

DON GINO

Hey Carmine, settle down. These guys have the oil, weapons, poppy fields and heavy connections. So leave it alone tonight. We all made a truce -- no one is taking over anybody.

MR. SUN

He's right, the last thing we want is to have is a financial crisis. The Bazins, the Russians, Mexicans, the Blacks, your associates and mine all made the deal.

CARMINE

I don't like this financial truce crap. It stinks. You can't trust those Arabs, they don't keep their word. They'll screw us over, the first chance they get.

DON GINO

That may be. We'll keep an eye on 'em, is all. We'll talk about this at the meeting tomorrow. Til then try and enjoy yourself, it's too pretty of a night to waste worrying.

Carmine looks bilious. But he heeds his brother.

EXT. BEVERLY HILTON HOTEL - LATER
Ken and Maggie take a break out on the patio.

KEN

Do you want to? You know...

MAGGIE

Ken, you know what my father will say.

KEN

I don't care, I love you. Ever since I lost my family, you are the only one in my life.

Maggie's lost in thought.

KEN (CONT'D)

What's wrong?

MAGGIE

My father... he's not what you think he is. He likes you, he thinks of you as a son. But us? Married? He's not going to go for that idea.

KEN

Whatever your father does for a living, it's doesn't matter. He'll approve of us. Let him give it a chance.

Tommy, weaving and drunk, appears. He sees Maggie, smiles, and barges in.

TOMMY
(to Ken)

Hey you... fuck off.

Tommy pushes Ken roughly to the ground, and turns to Maggie. He turns on his lame charm.

TOMMY (CONT'D)

Hey baby! Wanna have some fun? How about a little kiss?

He starts pawing her. Maggie resists.

MAGGIE

Jesus, get off me! You creep!

TOMMY

You know you want it!

Ken gets up and confronts Tommy.

                    KEN

She said get off of her!

Ken and Tommy get into a shoving match.

                    TOMMY

Don't touch me! Nobody touches me! Especially a
Chink like you!

                    KEN

You touch her, I'll break every bone in your body.
You'll piss blood for a year.

                    TOMMY

Fuck you!

Tommy whips aside his coat, revealing his 9mm.

                    JIMMY (O.S.)

Tommy!!!

Out of nowhere, Jimmy and two of his boys take hold of Tommy. Tommy struggles. He flips Ken the bird.
    Mr. Sun, Zan and Tai watch from the shadows.

                    JIMMY (CONT'D)
                    (to Ken and Maggie)

Sorry.

                    (to Tommy)

What the hell are you trying to do? You're ruining
everything.

TOMMY
Just trying to keep her company.

Jimmy slaps Tommy's face. He reddens in embarrassment.

JIMMY
Never touch another man's woman. You know that. It's
fucking disrespectful.
(to his boys)
Get him outta here!

The boys drag Tommy off.

KEN
Thanks, Jimmy.

JIMMY
No problem. He's drunk. Dumb asshole. I'll talk with
him when I go home. I'm real sorry about this.

KEN
Don't be. Not your fault. It's cool.

Jimmy smiles and leaves.
Mr. Sun, Zan and Tai walk up. Ken and Maggie regard them with surprise.

MR. SUN
(to Maggie)
Time to go home.

He nods to Zan and Tai, who escort her out. She looks apologetically back at
Ken as she goes.

KEN

Mr. Sun, I didn't start this, I was--

MR. SUN
(coldly)
Thank you for protecting my daughter.

Ken sees talking's no use. He nods and leaves. Johnny drifts up behind. Mr. Sun looks at him.

JOHNNY

I don't think Ken would fit well into our special organization.

MR. SUN

Don't worry. He's a schoolboy. A good earner. We'll keep an eye on him. Just make sure my daughter is well protected.

JOHNNY

Yes, sir.

EXT. MONTEREY PARK, CA - DAY
Ken drives his car down N. Garfield. The signs all advertise Asian businesses. Many Asians can be seen walking the streets.

EXT. MING HOUSE - DAY
Ken walks up the front walk and knocks on the door. It's answered by his aunt Mei. She's somewhat happy to see him.

INT. MING HOUSE - DAY
Greetings all around from his uncle Wen and cousin Hung.

MEI

How you been Ken?

KEN

Doing good. Working at the art gallery's the best career decision I ever made...

WEN
(in Chinese)

At least you are working.

KEN

How's everything with you?

MEI

Everything is good. Your cousin made full detective!

Ken turns to Hung, impressed.

KEN

That's great! Where?

HUNG

Downtown. Robbery-Homicide.

KEN

Impressive. The heart of the beast.

HUNG

Pretty much.

Ken gives him a handshake and a half-hug. Over his cousin's shoulder, his eyes
are nervous.

INT. MING HOUSE - LATER

The remains of a sumptuous dinner lie on the table. The little group is stuffed.

                    KEN

          I miss my family. I wish they were here. Especially
          Dad. He would have been proud of me.

Mei and Wen exchange glances. No sympathy in their eyes.

               KEN (CONT'D)

          What?

                    MEI

          No disrespect, but it's very hard for me to mourn my
          brother's passing. Given his disgraceful reputation--

                    KEN

          I don't believe that, my father was an honest cop! Like
          Hung here!

Mei, Hung and Wen are silent.

               KEN (CONT'D)

          What are you not telling me?

                    MEI

          I hoped I wouldn't have to -- but your father was not
          an honest cop.

                    KEN

          What are you talking about?

WEN
(in Chinese)
Hung, I need your help with something.

HUNG
Sure, Pop.

They exit. Leaving Ken and Wen alone.

MEI
Your father was on the Tongs' payroll. When he became a Tong in the syndicate. He did some bad things.

KEN
Come on...

MEI
Listen to me, Ken. The reason your father came to
America was because he was fleeing for his life. He
embezzled ten million Chinese yuan. He betrayed the
Tongs... and your grandfather was killed because of it.

Ken realizes.

KEN
That's how he paid for the shop. The house. Harvard...

MEI
Your education was financed by Tong money. Blood
money.

Ken is bowled over.

KEN

So _that's_ why they were murdered. What about my grandfather?

MEI

Liu Chow Fei, your grandfather, was a bookie and rack-eteer. Your grandmother worked with him in his operations helping him in his criminal career. I was ashamed to be part of our family. It disgusts me even now.

Ken sits back, still astonished at the information.

KEN

Aunt Mei, regardless what they did, I think they did this because they wanted to help all of us...

Mei explodes with rage.

MEI

I don't need that kind of help! I am better off without them! We work for our living, Uncle Wen and my son are my family! Your father and grandfather brought shame to this family and got everyone killed. He was an evil man and your mother was a fool to fall in love with him.

She calms her emotions. But she points at him, her manner severe.

MEI (CONT'D)

Please, do not bring this up again. If you do, we will not speak to you again. You will be dead to us.

KEN

But surely Mr. Sun--

As soon as Mei hears Mr. Sun's name, she points to the door.

                    MEI
          Leave. Now. Get out!

Ken is startled.

                    KEN
          Aunt Mei...

Aunt Mei turns her back to Ken.

                    MEI
          I said get out!

Ken quietly leaves

EXT. MING HOUSE - MOMENTS LATER
Hung exits and crosses to Ken at his car.

                    KEN
          Hung, is it true? What she said?

                    HUNG
          It's true.

                    KEN
          I don't believe her. Why is she upset with Dad and
          Grandfather? Hell, she threw me out when I men-
          tioned Mr. Sun's name...

                    HUNG
          Mr. Zao Sun?

Ken nods.

> HUNG (CONT'D)
> Ken, Zao Sun runs this city. San Gabriel, Chinatown,
> Koreatown, Little Tokyo and Monterey Park. That's all
> his. He's well known at the department -- he's a very
> dangerous man.

> KEN
> Dangerous? How?

Hung can't bring himself to reveal the truth.

> HUNG
> He's a very powerful man, Ken. Listen, this is why I
> chose to become a cop. We all worked hard to get away
> from this shit, away from our family history.

> KEN
> So did I.

> HUNG
> Just be careful. And call me if anyone gives you any
> trouble.

Hung hands Ken his business card. Ken nods, gives Hung a hug, and gets into his car.

INT. GAS STATION BATHROOM - DAY (BACK TO PRESENT)
Ken has finished salving his wounds, and cleaning up. He looks at himself in the mirror.

KEN (V.O.)

I should have listened to Hung when I had the chance.
Little did I know that was going along for the ride... a
long ride.

FLASHBACK MONTAGE
SUPER: "2006"
Dressed to kill, Ken presses the flesh at a fancy party.

KEN (V.O.)

It was the high life. I was making friends with celebrities, billionaires, the best of the best.

In the art gallery office, Ken laughs with his crew -- Benny, Mike Lee, Johnny,
Zan and Tai.

KEN (V.O.) (CONT'D)

My buddy Mike was helping out on the legal end. The
rest of us were hitting on all cylinders. Investments,
movies, no matter what we did, it turned to gold.

In the Electric Alley, a dance club, Ken and Maggie dance with Jimmy and his
girl. Some of the other Malone and Sun siblings are there as well, having fun.

KEN (V.O.) (CONT'D)

We even started a couple of nightclubs. The Electric
Alley and the White Tiger Supper Club. They quickly
became the hottest tickets in town.

The entourage also parties at the White Tiger Jazz Supper Club. They smoke ci-
gars at a posh table with lots of expensive Chinese food and liquor. A band plays
cool Hip-Hop and R&B.

> KEN (V.O.) (CONT'D)
>
> There was Jimmy, Mike, Johnny and me. Zan and Tai. Benny. We were the true bosses of LA. Everything belonged to us. We loved it. Clubs, cocktails, fast cars, and hot women. So much excess it would make you more high than bare naked ladies serving champagne.

The group dances with various girls. Behind them the MC sings Luther Vandross & Barry White songs.

> KEN (V.O.) (CONT'D)
>
> This was the dream. The life I always wanted and now I finally got it. Sometimes I saw or heard things that made me nervous... but I just put it out of my mind. It was better than the all those poor suckers out there, who worked shitty jobs for piss pay and worrying about paying their rent. They had no guts, we did whatever we wanted, we took whatever wanted. The world was ours.

Maggie and Ken dance at the Electric Alley.

> KEN (V.O.) (CONT'D)
>
> It would've been nothing at all, though... without Maggie.

INT. ART GALLERY - AFTERNOON

Johnny, Zan, Tai and Benny sit around a large table.

> JOHNNY
>
> Well guys I got some good news. Big Billy Ramon is back in town. He's putting on a birthday party at a mansion. Booze, broads, coke... Everything you want.

ZAN

Big Billy? Shit, I haven't seen him in ages. We're there man!

Ken walks in. The boys greet him.

JOHNNY

Hey Ken, you want to roll with us to a party? It'll be a lot of fun.

KEN

I'd like to but I've got to catch up on work.

JOHNNY

Come on -- you've been working all week. And at night you're with Maggie. Come party with your boys! Get out of the office and have a life.

ZAN

Yeah, man -- gotta get some strange pussy. Find out what you've been missing!

KEN

I don't--

JOHNNY

Listen, just come out with us. Do we have to say please?

KEN

Alright, alright.

The boys cheer.

INT. SHERMAN OAKS MANSION - DAY

Ken, Johnny, Zan, Tai and Benny -- dressed to the nines --- enter Big Billy's party. The mansion's filled to the rafters with celebs, musicians, scantily clad (even naked) girls.

In the corners, flashy characters hold court. Through open doorways, mountains of coke are enjoyed by wired individuals. Hip-Hop music is playing.

Their host, BIG BILLY RAMON, 40, a heavy-set mulatto American, circulates. Think Suge Knight mixed with Rick Ross.

> KEN (V.O.)
> Big Billy Ramon was a main man in the music industry.
> The kind of guy you liked immediately and everybody
> liked Big Billy. Anything you wanted, he could get it for
> you. And I do mean anything. He was the head presi-
> dent of Phat Kat Records, one of the biggest hip hop
> labels on the west coast.

> ZAN
> Shit, we gotta go to more of these parties.

> TAI
> Hell yeah!

Ken looks a bit nervous.

> BENNY
> Ken, what's up?

> KEN
> I never been to a party like this. Why are we here?

Johnny orders up some shots. Ken stares around the place at the larger-than-life characters.

> ### KEN (V.O.) (CONT'D)
> Those feelings I had... they were starting to get stronger. There was something wrong with the company I was keeping...

EXT. SHERMAN OAKS MANSION - POOL - DAY
Ken drifts around the pool.

> ### KEN (V.O.)
> Everybody was there. Lawyers, politicians...

A silver-haired gentleman laughs with some cronies...

> ### KEN (V.O.) (CONT'D)
> The Chief of Police...

Nearby, leathery-tanned dudes in shades hang out with bubbly blondes with huge boobs, tottering on stiletto heels.

> ### KEN (V.O.) (CONT'D)
> ...rubbing shoulders with porn moguls and their girls...

Ken looks doubtful.

> ### KEN (V.O.) (CONT'D)
> It was making me uneasy. I had – a really bad vibe about being here. I should not have come.

Ken comes upon Zan, Tai and Benny partying at the pool. Johnny's there too -- he drags Ken over to Big Billy. Jimmy Malone's there too. He nods hello to Ken.

> ### JOHNNY
> Big Billy!

They shake hands.

BIG BILLY
Yo brother, how you been?

JOHNNY
Alright. This party is the bomb! Best bash you put on yet.

JIMMY
Damn straight. Pussy, everywhere you look. Only Big Billy can put up a spread like this, that's for sure.

BIG BILLY
That's right. Best keep your mind on your work, and not your dick.

Jimmy chuckles. It's a bit strained, though.

JOHNNY
Big Billy, this is my boy Ken Liu -- one of our associates.

Ken shakes hands with Big Billy Ramon.

KEN
Nice to meet you.

BIG BILLY
I heard about you -- you're Mr. Sun's moneymaker.

KEN
Yeah, I guess so.

BIG BILLY

Man, If it wasn't for Mr. Sun and Mr. Malone. I wouldn't even be where I'm at.

KEN

Whose birthday is it?

BIG BILLY

This heiress. Her rich daddy paid for all this. Her name is Deja.

KEN

Who is Deja?

BIG BILLY

Jesus, don't they let you outta the house? She's got more money than all the Kardashians combined.

KEN

Who?

Big Billy sees someone else, and he's off in full meet-and-greet mode. Jimmy grins, trails after.

Zan, Tai and Benny join Ken and Johnny.

ZAN

I heard that the birthday girl is a model.

TAI

I heard she's an actress.

BENNY

I heard she's a porn star.

JOHNNY

Well, she did that sex tape, so I guess she's all three. A fucking slut all in one.

The boys laugh. Then the DJ makes an announcement.

DJ

Everybody having a good time? Make some noise! Aw yeah!

The crowd cheers, and our boys cheer along.

DJ (CONT'D)

A big shout-out to our sponsors for putting this killer bash together! And now... please welcome... the birth-day girl herself -- Deja Bazin!

ZARIA "DEJA" BAZIN, 25, tan, pampered, total bombshell, booms out in a skin-tight, shiny purple ensemble. The crowd cheers.

Ken stares. Deja starts dancing to the music. Guys and girls. She waves to the crowd.

KEN (V.O.)

When I laid my eyes on her, I knew she was trouble. But holy shit, what a goddess!

Ken shakes it off, suddenly guilty.

KEN (V.O.) (CONT'D)

What was I thinking? I loved Maggie. I wouldn't cheat on her. Still...

He stares again at Deja, with lust in his eyes.

KEN (V.O.) (CONT'D)
...what a woman. Smoking.

Johnny, however, doesn't look happy.

JOHNNY
I think we should leave.

ZAN
What the hell's the matter, we just got here!

JOHNNY
C'mon, goddammit.

Johnny turns to pull Ken toward the door -- but Jimmy intercepts them.

JIMMY
Leaving so soon?

JOHNNY
I didn't know this was going to be a Bazin party.

JIMMY
Relax -- there's a truce. None of that tonight. Big Billy
and I are handling this. Stay, enjoy yourselves, and just
kick back man. Have a drink.

Zan, Tai and Benny stare as Deja swirls by them. They make comments, she
flirts back. But she keeps going.

ZAN
Shit, she is fine.

                            TAI
          She's got beauty and booty.

Benny whistles. Jimmy waves his hand in warning.

                           JIMMY
          Be careful around her -- she's like a tiger that can't be
          tamed. That girl's got serious issues.

                           BENNY
          How do you know that?

                           JIMMY
          Because I hit that, that's how. She drove me crazy,
          though. That girl can't keep it in her pants. She's a
          complete nymphomaniac, loves to live for sex and
          money. Stay away from her, she's no good.

Ken notices Tommy among the crowd. Deja swirls past him, gives him a lingering kiss.

INT. SHERMAN OAKS MANSION - LATER
A toilet FLUSHES. Ken comes out of a bathroom, adjusting his pants. He hears
a muffled male SCREAM.
     He stops at a cracked door and looks inside.
     BASSIM OMAR BAZIN, 30s, very handsome, and several henchmen have
a man tied to a chair. They're taking turns beating the shit out of him. Bassim
screams at the man in Armenian.
     The door slams shut. Ken quickly moves off.

EXT. SHERMAN OAKS MANSION - LATER
Ken goes outside to the bar to get a drink.

KEN (V.O.)
What I'd seen, I couldn't stop thinking about. But I had
to put it out of my head... just keep it cool.

Suddenly, Deja, big as life, appears next to him.

DEJA
Hey, sexy. How you doing?

KEN
I'm doing good. Happy birthday!

DEJA
Aw, thank you.

KEN
(to Bartender)
Yo. Vodka Martini. Dry.
(to Deja)
What can I get you?

DEJA
Same.

The bartender whips up two, and delivers them with a flourish. Ken and Deja
drink.

DEJA (CONT'D)
You're new here. I haven't seen you around town.

KEN
Yeah, I've been working a lot.

Deja grabs his drink. Puts them both on the bar.

                    DEJA
        All work and no play...

She pulls him out onto the dance floor. Ken has no choice but to follow along. Deja dances him seductively. More like a stripper than anything else. Ken struggles to be respectable.

                    KEN
        Listen, I have a girlfriend.

                    DEJA
        She here? Come on, dance with me.

Ken shakes his head. Deja smiles and pulls him onto the floor.
    Tommy passes by the dance floor, and notices Deja with Ken. He crosses to them and grabs Deja away from Ken.

                DEJA (CONT'D)
        Hey, what the fuck!

                    KEN
        What's your problem?

                    TOMMY
        What's my problem? You're my fucking problem!

Deja wrests her arm from Tommy's grasp.

                TOMMY (CONT'D)
        You know who I am? What I could do to you? What I
        could have done to you? Don't fuck with me, Chink.

                    DEJA
Go easy on him, Tommy.

                    TOMMY
Shut up.

Deja clearly enjoys being talked to like this. But Ken doesn't get that.

                    KEN
Hey, show some respect! She's a lady.

                    TOMMY
Respect? Face it, Ken -- you wouldn't have fuck all if
it wasn't for my family and your boss. Respect? You
chow mein prick, you should be showing it to me!

                    KEN
               (grabs crotch)
Respect this.

Jimmy appears, gets between them.

                    JIMMY
Hey, hey, hey!
               (laughs)
What the fuck! Quit playin' around you guys.

                    TOMMY
Fine. C'mon, Deja, time for you birthday fuck.

Tommy tries to pick her up off the ground, but Deja wrestles around with him
and winds up hauling him away.

Jimmy puts his hands on Ken's shoulders.

                    JIMMY
          Settle down, man. It's alright.

                    KEN
          Why do you put up with that asshole?

                    JIMMY
          He's my brother. I have to. He thinks he's a big shot --
          we let him think that. There's no changing him. He's
          just had a silver spoon up his ass all his life.

                    KEN
          You're his brother -- same spoon's been up your ass
          too, right?

Jimmy's eyes flash, but he takes it good-naturedly.

                    JIMMY
          I suppose. Maybe I just got all the good genes.

He starts steering Ken away from the staring people, who've already forgotten
what happened.

                    JIMMY (CONT'D)
          Trust me -- I work very hard, unlike my brother. In
          business, we cooperate. You and I know that. Tommy,
          he can't figure that out.

INT. SHERMAN OAKS MANSION - STAIRS - DAY
As she's pulled up the stairs by Tommy, Deja looks down at the entryway.
     Ken and Jimmy laugh, shake hands. Ken leaves.
     Deja watches Ken thoughtfully. Tommy yanks her into the bedroom.

KEN (V.O.)

Some people aren't looking for anything more than a cheap thrill. I wanted more than that.

EXT. MR. SUN'S BACKYARD - DAY

Mr. Sun's home features a lush, vibrant and well-trim backyard, complete with a koi pond, a Buddha shrine, and several stone statues of Asian dragons hidden among the bamboo trees and shrubs. In the center of the garden is a white gazebo where Ken and Maggie are getting married. In front of the gazebo, the entire extended family is in attendance. Everyone is dressed in their best, and smiling as Ken and Maggie are married. A Christian minister and a Buddhist lama offer their blessings.

KEN (V.O.)

And eventually, I did find exactly what I was looking for.

A reception follows, and everyone is celebrating. Plenty of food and drinks are provided, and there is a massive wedding cake that Ken and Maggie start cutting. There are also mountains of wedding presents from the family. Mr. Sun embraces Ken warmly.

MR. SUN

Congratulations, Ken.

KEN

Thank you, Mr. Sun. I promise I'll take good care of her.

MR. SUN

Don't call me Mr. Sun anymore, you can call me father. Remember: a man of integrity is always loyal to his wife and family.

> KEN
>
> Does that include the extended family?

Mr. Sun laughs.

> MR. SUN
>
> Of course.

SERIES OF SHOTS

Ken is at a family party in a high-class restaurant. Family members from all different nationalities gather at a fully-laden table. Ken sits between Maggie and Jimmy, eating, drinking and laughing.

> KEN (V.O.)
>
> My new family was amazing, and we shared every special moment together as one. It was interesting to be around so many diverse cultures, but what really made it special was my best friend and my wife.

Jimmy passes a tray of food to Ken, who fills up his plate. He then passes it to Maggie.

> KEN (V.O.) (CONT'D)
>
> It seemed like another lifetime when I lost my parents, and now things were completely different for me. The future looked brighter than I ever could've imagined.

INT. ART GALLERY - NIGHT

Super: "Two Weeks Later"

Ken and Maggie hold court at a sumptuous event.

> KEN (V.O.)
>
> Later that night, Maggie and I hosted the annual gala at the gallery.

NIKKI SUN, mid 20s, Mr. Sun's youngest daughter, a fashion model and social-ite, giggles with her sister.

> KEN (V.O.) (CONT'D)
> It was the biggest exhibit in town and anyone on the
> list, attended. Including Maggie's younger sister Nikki,
> a model and beautiful socialite herself.

Along with the Hollywood celebrities are a number of local "business" figures -- ALEX GOMEZ, 40s, and his mistress, along with his Mexican Mafia allies. SERGEI DIMITRI, 60s, head of the Russian mob. HAN MURIMOTO, 60s, head of the Yakuza. Big Billy's there, along this his Westside Syndicate. And even... the Bazins...

> KEN (V.O.) (CONT'D)
> We had buyers everywhere, including a certain Persian
> businessman and his family.

Deja hangs on the arm of her father, patriarch ASIM DAVARI BAZIN, 60s. Also there, Bassim. Who we last saw kicking the shit out of someone.

> KEN (V.O.) (CONT'D)
> Asim Davari Bazin. Billionaire head of the Bazin fam-
> ily. A major captain of industry. He bought half of the
> artwork that night. He reminded me of the story of
> Midas. The man with the golden touch.

Bassim shakes Ken's hand. Ken smiles nervously.

INT. ART GALLERY - LATER
Party's over. Ken and Maggie gather their things, and look through papers de-tailing the deals made.

JOHNNY
Hey, Ken, Maggie, I'll meet you both outside.

MAGGIE
We'll meet you at the restaurant for dinner.

Johnny leaves the art gallery. Ken moves toward the back office. He turns to Maggie.

KEN
Hey Maggie, -- could you give me a hand for a minute?

MAGGIE
Sure, sweetie, one sec.

Ken goes into the office.

Maggie checks some papers, puts them down and moves to join him.

Suddenly, a group of SKI-MASKED ROBBERS storm into the gallery and seize Maggie. Masked Robber #1 holds a gun to her head.

MASKED ROBBER #1
Alright bitch, don't make a sound or you're dead. Now open the fuckin' vault, nice and easy.

MAGGIE
It's back there. I don't have the key.

Masked Robber #1 roughly checks her pockets -- copping a feel along the way. He shakes his head.

The others move to the vault and slap C4 on it. Masked Robber #2 is clearly a woman -- big boobs. Kind of familiar, how bodacious she is... Maggie notices. Recognition dawns.

They hook up detonators, and take cover --

BOOM! The vault blows open.

INT. ART GALLERY - OFFICE - NIGHT
Ken jumps up. He peeks through the window, sees the robbers.
    He whips out his phone. Texts to Johnny: "Emergency, call cops!"

INT. ART GALLERY - NIGHT
The robbers transfer cash to a van waiting just outside.

                    MASKED ROBBER #1
        Hurry it up!

Maggie recognizes the voice.

                        MAGGIE
        Tommy.

Masked Robber #1 looks at her.

                    MAGGIE (CONT'D)
        You'll never get away with it, Tommy.

Maggie elbows Tommy's stomach -- attempts to escape.
    Tommy falls down -- but shoots her in the back.

INT. ART GALLERY - OFFICE - NIGHT
Ken watches in horror.

                        KEN
        Bastards!

Ken runs out of the office.

INT. ART GALLERY - OFFICE - NIGHT
Ken runs right toward them. The robbers freeze momentarily, surprised at the
incursion.

Ken punches Tommy, turns and kicks another. A bag of money goes flying. Beating him senseless.

He turns toward Maggie -- Masked Shooter #2 shoots him.

Ken falls back, bleeding copiously. Shot in the shoulder.

Tommy gets up.

> TOMMY
>
> C'mon, someone's coming. Let's go!

The boys retrieve the money and run outside. Tommy brings up the rear. He sneers down at Ken.

He aims at Ken's head. The moment he squeezes off a shot, Maggie grabs his ankle.

The shot goes wide. The sound of cars ROARING closer outside.

Tommy wrests his foot from her weak grasp and runs outside. He and his boys speed off.

Ken goes to Maggie. Still barely alive.

> MAGGIE
>
> Ken...It was... Tommy... and...

> KEN
>
> Maggie...

Ken loses consciousness.

Johnny arrives and sees Maggie and Ken wounded.

INT. LOS ANGELES HOSPITAL - DAY

Ken, heavily bandaged, wakes up. At his bedside, Mikey, Zan, Tai and Benny.

> KEN
>
> Maggie?

The boys look uncomfortable. Johnny sidles up. Puts her wedding ring into Ken's hand.

Ken lays back. He cries.

INT. GAS STATION BATHROOM - DAY (BACK TO PRESENT)
Ken looks at the same ring, in the palm of his hand. The wound is still fresh.

> KEN (V.O.)
> I never fully recovered after Maggie's death. The past caught up with me again. I couldn't understand why everyone I loved ended up dying.

FLASHBACK - INT. MR. SUN'S OFFICE - DAY
The Suns and Malones (without Tommy) sit together around a table. Johnny Wu stands behind Mr. Sun.

> MR. SUN
> (to Don Gino)
> I want to know what this is all about.

Mr. Sun looks dangerous as Death himself.

> MR. SUN (CONT'D)
> With her dying breath, my Maggie said "Tommy".

> JOHNNY
> Whoever the hell shot her, deserves to die.

The Malones exchange uncomfortable glances.

> DON GINO
> Mr. Sun. We're business partners, family. We'd never sanction such a thing.

JIMMY

It has to be Tommy. He was always trying to put the move on her.

Don Gino looks sharply at him.

DON GINO

I don't believe it. As much as my youngest son is a scum bag. He would never harm one of us. Much less kill a member of our extended family.

JIMMY

Tommy is out of control and now he's gone too goddamn far.

Don Gino shakes his head sadly. He always knew it'd come to this.

MR. SUN

I want justice for my daughter.

DON GINO

Zao... I'll take care of it personally. No one needs to know.

MR. SUN

I need to know. Otherwise, our business arrangement -- and friendship -- will be at an end.

JOHNNY

This meeting is adjourned.

He turns his chair away. The meeting is over. The Malones get up and leave.

EXT. GREEN HILLS CEMETERY - DAY

Maggie's laid to rest in a private somber ceremony. The Suns and their entourage are all present.

Nikki weeps next to Mr. Sun.

Ken watches, his face hard.

                         KEN (V.O.)
          I swore to myself that day... I would not rest until
          Tommy was dead. If the Malones couldn't or wouldn't
          take care of him... then I would.

EXT. GREEN HILLS CEMETERY - DAY

Ken follows the mourners to their cars. Two people in black trench coats fall in step with him. AGENT BRIGGS and AGENT RAMIREZ, 30s. Briggs is a blond, skinny man. Ramirez is a dark Hispanic woman.

                         AGENT BRIGGS
          Mr. Ken Liu?

Ken nods.

                         AGENT BRIGGS (CONT'D)
          Agent Briggs, FBI. This is Agent Ramirez. We would
          like to ask you a few questions.

                         KEN
          Some other time, perhaps.

Ken leaves.

                         AGENT RAMIREZ
          We'll be watching you!

INT. KEN'S PENTHOUSE APARTMENT - DAY

Ken's sits drinking a glass of scotch and smoking a cigarette. He takes a puff, and crushes it out.

A sudden spasm of sadness overwhelms him. He buries his face in his arms.

When his face reappears, it's stone cold. He glances at a picture on the table. Maggie and him, laughing in the sun.

Rage builds. He suddenly hurls the scotch to shatter against the wall.

His cell rings. It rings again. Finally, he looks at it.

"PRIVATE NUMBER" reads the display. Curious, he answers.

                    KEN
          Hello.

                    DEJA (V.O.)
          Ken.

                    KEN
          Deja! How'd you get this number?

                    DEJA (V.O.)
          I heard about your wife's death. I just want to say I'm
          sorry.

                    KEN
          Thanks Deja. I appreciate your concern. But if Tommy
          found out you talked to me, he'd kill us both.

                    DEJA (V.O.)
          Don't worry about him. He's with his boyfriends.

                    KEN
          What? Where?

DEJA (V.O.)

I don't know.

KEN

Why the hell are you with him?

DEJA (V.O.)

He's good in the bedroom.

KEN

But he treats you like he owns you.

DEJA (V.O.)

Maybe. But it's better than guys too scared of even approaching me. Like you perhaps.

KEN

Deja, I just lost my wife. That's not funny.

DEJA (V.O.)

I'm sorry. I get over carried sometimes.

KEN (CONT'D)

There's got to be more to it than that.

DEJA (V.O.)
(sighs)

He's not like everyone else in his family. He's independent, he's got plans for himself, and I've always liked that about him.

KEN

He's a murderer. He killed my wife.

DEJA (V.O.)

Can't be -- Tommy was with me on the night of the murder.

KEN

She identified him with her dying breath!

DEJA (V.O.)

She said 'Tommy Malone'?

KEN

Just 'Tommy'.

DEJA

Then maybe it's some other Tommy? Listen, Ken, I gotta go. Whoever did this, I hope he gets what's coming. I'm sorry for your loss.

She hangs up. Ken stares at the phone.

INT. DIVE BAR - NIGHT

Ken sits in a dark booth, disheveled, wasted, chain-smoking.

KEN

I went downhill fast. I still kept up appearances... mostly. But inside, nothing but vengeance was keeping me going.

A waitress brings scotch. He drinks up.

KEN (V.O.) (CONT'D)

The money was no longer making me happy and the lifestyle meant nothing to me. I tried to date new women... but none of them were Maggie.

Suddenly, he hears a familiar voice.

> TOMMY (O.S.)
> I know I fucked up by shooting the bitch.

Ken's eyes almost pop out of his head. He leans back to hear.

From another angle, we see what he can't -- Tommy's in the next booth with some unfamiliar men we don't see.

> MYSTERY PERSON (O.S.)
> You were only supposed to rob the goddamn place.
> Not kill anyone.

> TOMMY
> I got caught up in the heat of the moment.

> MYSTERY PERSON (O.S.)
> So I now have to clean up your fuck ups. I hear your
> own family's looking for you.

> TOMMY
> They'll never do anything. Business is business, but
> blood's blood. They're not gonna grease me over one
> dead bitch.

> MYSTERY PERSON (O.S.)
> If they find out you did this, they'll also find out your
> other plans.

> TOMMY
> Just stay cool, alright? I'll get out of town soon. They'll
> never find me.

Ken slips out of the booth unseen.

INT. MING HOUSE - DAY

Hung talks on the phone, watching for his mother.

> KEN (V.O.)
>
> Did you find anything out?

> HUNG
>
> I did the best I could, but...

> KEN (V.O.)
>
> But what...

> HUNG
>
> The forensic evidence was botched. I think someone paid them off to destroy it. Without that evidence, we've got nothing. I'm sorry.

> KEN (V.O.)
>
> Hung, I can't let them get away with this. Can you help me or not?!

> HUNG
>
> Listen, don't do anything stupid. Okay? Please, it's not worth it.

INT. KEN'S APARTMENT - DAY

Ken nods.

> KEN
>
> Okay.

His hands, however, are fiddling with a shiny new .38.

> HUNG (V.O.)
> I'll let you know if I hear anything. Are you gonna be okay?

> KEN
> Yeah. I'll be fine.

He hangs up. Flips out the cylinder. The gun's fully loaded. Hollow points. He whips it closed, and slips it in his pocket.

INT. GUN RANGE - DAY
Ken practices firing his gun at the local firing range. His aim is sloppy.

Two stalls down, Jimmy fires. Reloading, he notices Ken. He crosses over to him.

> JIMMY
> Hey Ken, how you doing buddy?

> KEN
> Oh hey, Jimmy. Not so good. My aim sucks today.

> JIMMY
> Better than drinking your blues away, like you been doing.

Ken glances at him. Nods slowly.

> JIMMY (CONT'D)
> I like to come down here to blast a few rounds now and then. Helps work off the tension. Been a lot of that lately.

Ken fires but misses.

                         KEN
Shit!

                         JIMMY
        You gotta breathe into it. Let it be an extension of your
        arm. Let me show you.

INT. GUN RANGE - LATER
From behind a target, we see a hole appear dead center. Five more shots -- the
center's torn open. Through the hole, we see Ken lower the smoking gun. He
and Jimmy grin.

EXT. GUN RANGE PARKING LOT - DAY
The two stand by their cars, having a smoke.

                         KEN
        Ever since the robbery and Maggie getting killed... I
        figured it'd be best to leave.

                         JIMMY
        Yeah. She was a great girl.

                         KEN
        Any word on Tommy?

                         JIMMY
        He's gone. No trace.

                         KEN
        You wouldn't lie to me?

Jimmy looks Ken straight in the eye.

                         JIMMY
         No.

Ken doesn't believe Jimmy. But he's got to let it go.

INT. KEN'S CAR - DAY
Ken drives, his face tormented.
    He plays "Juicy" by The Notorious B.I.G. on the radio.

                       KEN (V.O.)
         I was pretty sure Jimmy wouldn't give him up. "Blood's
         blood", like Tommy said. I figured I'd have to hunt him
         down myself... but I had no idea where to start.

Ken's phone rings. "Unknown Name" shows on the display.

                       KEN (CONT'D)
         Hello?

                  FEMALE VOICE (V.O.)
         I know the location of your wife's killer.

                         KEN
         Who is this?

                  FEMALE VOICE (V.O.)
         Shut up and listen. First, you gotta suit up. I know this
         isn't your line of work, so I got a guy who can help you.
         Meet him at the Dornsey Hotel downtown. Room 22.

                         KEN
         Listen, if you think--

> FEMALE VOICE (V.O.)
> That man hurt my family too. I want payback. Once you've picked up the stuff, I'll text you the address where he's hiding.

The female caller hangs up.

Ken stares at it in confusion. He thinks a moment, then hits the accelerator.

EXT. DORNSEY HOTEL - NIGHT

Ken pulls up to a seedy hotel in the mean streets of Downtown L.A. He glances up at the windows, uncertain what he might find.

INT. DORNSEY HOTEL HALLWAY - NIGHT

Ken walks up and knocks on the door of Room 22.

> VOICE (O.S.)
> Who is it?

> KEN
> A lady sent me.

The door opens up and Ken hesitantly goes inside.

> KEN (V.O.) (CONT'D)
> Turned out the guy was a weapons dealer. And he wasn't in it for charity. I forked over a couple thousand. But hey, in for a penny...

Moments later, Ken reemerges with a suitcase.

> KEN (V.O.) (CONT'D)
> He knew who my anonymous tipster was, but he wouldn't tell me.

SERIES OF SHOTS
Ken parks in a dark alley.

KEN (V.O.)

I was about to take a human life. And dressed for the part.

Ken opens the briefcase on the hood of the car.
Ken straps on a Kevlar vest.
Two pistols with silencers go in a pair of shoulder holsters.
A black trench coat swirls around him as he puts it on.
Black gloves on his hands...
Black sunglasses complete the ensemble.
Ken Liu... assassin... ready to raise some hell.

KEN (V.O.) (CONT'D)

I didn't think what it would mean. To kill a man. My heart was too full of vengeance. All I knew was, Tommy was better off dead, for what it was worth, the world would be a better place without scumbags like him. He was dirt, the only thing he belonged in was a body bag.

Ken gets a text. He looks at the display. Nods. Gets in the car.

INT. TOMMY'S APARTMENT - NIGHT
The place is a dump. Tommy, along with three of his henchmen, eats a late supper of takeout pizza and beer.
Tommy's on his cell.

TOMMY

Deja, you got the stuff for me to get out of town?

Tommy snorts a line of coke off a hip-hop CD case.

                    DEJA (V.O.)
It's all set. A guy will drop it off. He'll take care of you
and make sure the Chinese won't get you. Don't worry
about it.

                    TOMMY
                    (pissed)
I'm not worried, goodbye.

He sniffs.

INT. SHERMAN OAKS MANSION - NIGHT
Deja hangs up, with a snarl. She dials a number. Waits.

                    DEJA
Yeah, it's all set. When our fall guy kills Tommy, take
him out. Then maybe we can start moving some of our
art gallery cash.
                    (beat)
Yeah. Don't screw up.

She hangs up. She looks into the mirror. Just as beautiful as ever.

INT. APARTMENT HALLWAY - NIGHT
A pair of feet walks down a grim, dimly lit hallway in a cheap apartment complex.
A door marked "304" comes into view.
    Ken pauses. Does he have the sack to go through with it? He looks at his
hands. Can these hands kill a man?
    The hands curl into fists.

INT. TOMMY'S APARTMENT - NIGHT
There's a knock on the door.

TOMMY

That must be the guy. Bobby, go answer the door.

BOBBY, 30s, big fat and obese, walks to the peep hole and looks. He can't see anything... just some kind of black hole...

BOBBY

What the fuck?

INT. APARTMENT HALLWAY - NIGHT

The hole is Ken's pistol. He fires.

BULLET POV

The bullet exits the gun, penetrates the peephole, enters Bobby's eye, passes through his brain, and out the back -- in a shower of gore.

INT. TOMMY'S APARTMENT - NIGHT

Tommy and his goons jump up, shocked, as Bobby's large bulk tumbles to the floor with a loud thud.

In a split second, their guns are out and they're firing madly at the door. Swiss-cheesing it.

They cease firing. Nothing happens. No movement is seen through the holes.

INT. APARTMENT HALLWAY - NIGHT

Ken's head is turned to the side, in apparent agony. Is he shot? No, just stunned by the loud noise -- he's unharmed.

He lifts his leg and stomps on the ground. Making the kind of sound a body might make hitting the floor.

INT. APARTMENT - NIGHT

Tommy grins.

                    TOMMY
        Heh, got the fucker.

The boys, clustered together, move toward the door.

IT BURSTS OPEN
Ken appears, firing. Left, right, methodically.
        One henchman goes down immediately.
        Tommy grabs another, as a human shield. Several shots turn him into a corpse.
        Ken snarls in rage. He adjusts his aim. SHOOTS Tommy in the hand.

                    TOMMY (CONT'D)
            Aggh!

He drops the dead henchman and aims his pistol.
        Ken shoots it out of his hand.
        And puts a bullet in each leg, for good measure.
        Tommy falls to the floor, screaming. Only now does he seem to recognize the assailant.

                    TOMMY (CONT'D)
            You!!

Ken crosses the room -- Tommy goes for his gun, but Ken stomps on his hand. He presses his gun to Tommy's forehead.

                        KEN
            You killed her.

Tommy laughs.

TOMMY

So fuckin' what? The money was worth more than her life anyway. Just business, Ken. Go ahead, you fuckin' sore loser. Finish it.

KEN

Who else is involved? Who!

TOMMY

Your mother.

Ken smirks as he pulls the trigger. Painting the curtains red.

EXT. APARTMENT BUILDING - NIGHT
As Ken exits the building, shots ring out. Ricochet off the concrete.
    Ken races down to his car, jumps in and drives off.

EXT. KEN'S CAR - MOVING - NIGHT
Ken, excited, glances back, fearful -- no pursuit.

KEN (V.O.)

I finally got justice.

He relaxes. His wild eyes slowly settle. His face relaxes into a grin.

KEN (V.O.) (CONT'D)

But I wasn't completely satisfied. Something was missing.

INT. KEN'S APARTMENT - NIGHT
Ken sits on the couch in just his vest, holsters empty, drinking a beer. He does look relaxed. Only slightly troubled.
    The TV drones on. He suddenly sits up.

NEWSCASTER (V.O.)

Breaking news Downtown -- police have been called to an apartment complex where four men have been killed in a deadly shoot out. Early reports indicate one of the dead may be Thomas Malone. The Malone family has long been suspected to have extensive ties to organized crime...

This hits Ken like a ton of bricks.

KEN (V.O.)

Jesus Christ! The Malones were mobsters. How had I been so goddamn blind?

He jumps up and paces. The news drones on, unheard.

KEN (V.O.) (CONT'D)

I killed a gangster. I was totally fucked. The walls closed in on me. Like the coffin I'd soon be in...

Ken is losing his shit. He runs into the bedroom.

INT. KEN'S BEDROOM - MOMENTS LATER

Clothes fly out of drawers, and Ken stuffs them in a suitcase.

KEN (V.O.)

Auntie Mei, Uncle Wen and Cousin Hung were right. I was just falling into our families curse. I had to get the hell out of town.

Ken shoves too many clothes in his bag, pounds them hard to get them to fit. Then suddenly stops.

> KEN (V.O.) (CONT'D)

Then I realized. If Malone was a gangster... so was Mr. Sun. If I ran, I'd be screwing him too. And he had power... and influence.

Ken sits down heavily on the bed, thinking hard.

> KEN (V.O.) (CONT'D)

Running was no option. Mr. Sun was the only man who could help me.

INT. THRIFT STORE - DAY (BACK TO PRESENT)

Ken pays for a purchase. He's now wearing thrift store clothes, tags still hanging off them. He's dressed to blend in.

> KEN (V.O.)

The reality of what I had done... and the penalty I might have to pay... it was a hard weight. I let my anger get the best of me. And now I'd have to live with it for the rest of my life. And take whatever consequences there were.

Ken looks around, suspicious, and heads out of the store and down the sidewalk.

> KEN (V.O.) (CONT'D)

If I didn't do something, I'd be forever watching my back...

FLASHBACK - INT. MR. SUN'S OFFICE - NIGHT

Ken stands nervously before Mr. Sun.

> MR. SUN

Ken, you look like hell. You want something to drink?

                    KEN
          Dad... I've got a real problem.

                    MR. SUN
          Sit down, then, maybe I can help.

Ken sits down stiffly. He tries to gather the strength. It's difficult.
     Finally he just blurts it out.

                    KEN
          I killed a man tonight.

Mr. Sun raises his eyebrows. That's his only reaction.

                    KEN (CONT'D)
          It was Tommy.

Mr. Sun cocks his head. His face is otherwise impassive.

                    KEN (CONT'D)
          I got a tip to his location. And the gear. I suited up... I
          went in... and I killed him.

                    MR. SUN
          You're sure he's dead?

Ken nods.

                    MR. SUN (CONT'D)
          Good.

Ken blinks in surprise.

MR. SUN (CONT'D)

That is comforting news to hear. May he rot in hell where he belongs.

Ken just stares. Mr. Sun smiles. He stands and comes around the desk to Ken.

MR. SUN (CONT'D)

You're wondering why I'm not shocked? Scandalized? That kind of thing is for weaker men than we. We do what needs to be done. We identify a problem...
                    (claps his hands once)
...and we take care of it.

He puts his hand on Ken's shoulder.

MR. SUN (CONT'D)

That animal took my daughter from me. But now... now, it's like I've gained a son.

KEN
(worried and afraid)
What should I do? I'm not experienced... the police will find out it's me. They'll crucify me.

MR. SUN

Not necessarily.

KEN

I don't understand.

MR. SUN

I was hoping that in time I could introduce you to our family's true business. Now I know I can.

KEN

True business?

Mr. Sun pulls up his left sleeve. He shows Ken a dragon tattoo with a sun shape -- the symbol of the Triad family.

MR. SUN

This mark is a symbol of our clan and family's pride. The Order of the Sun. A secret underground society of thieves and assassins. We, and many others, are Triads, the Manchurian descendants of the old Heaven and Earth Society. This heritage has been in our family's bloodline for the last three hundred years.

KEN

Why didn't you tell me before?

MR. SUN

Because you were not yet ready to know. Now you are. I would like to welcome you to join our organization. You have already proved yourself to me in avenging my daughter's death.
(coldly)
The law is not justice. Only through vengeance, and the will to avenge... is justice truly served.
(beat)
Join us.

Ken's torn. He's at a major life crossroads.

KEN (V.O.)

It was a lot to take in. But I had lost the woman I loved. I had lost my parents, and could lose my freedom... and here was Mr. Sun... holding out a solution. A terrible, powerful solution.

Mr. Sun senses his hesitance. He puts his sleeve back down and squares to Ken. Putting his hands on both shoulders.

MR. SUN

Listen to me, son. I'm giving you this moment as an opportunity. If you choose to work for the Triad council, I can guarantee you complete immunity from the law.

KEN

How?

MR. SUN

Many judges and politicians work for us. Ours is a system of mutual expedience, respect, and silence.
(beat)
All you have to do is say yes, and join us.

Ken closes his eyes. He breathes deeply.

KEN

My parents, my wife...all of them were taken from me by gangs.

MR. SUN

That I know. I ordered the Tongs executed, to avenge Wong Fei and grant you peace.

Ken can't believe it. Sweat starts to bead on his brow. Mr. Sun keeps his composure.

> MR. SUN (CONT'D)
>
> Listen to me, Ken. Ours is a dangerous world. Beneath the facade of art galleries and parties, there is a world of smuggling, drugs and killings. But we take care of our own, and we have our own codes. You, however, have already involved yourself by killing Thomas Malone. If you join us, you will be protected, but if you refuse, you will be on your own, and I assure you, you will not make it.

Ken regains his composure, closing his eyes.

> KEN
>
> I'll join.

Mr. Sun smiles.

> MR. SUN
>
> Welcome home, son.

INT. INITIATION ROOM - NIGHT

Mr. Sun and several other high-ranking triad officers lead the initiation ceremony.

Ken stands in the center of the room before an altar. The altar is dedicated to Guan Yu, with incense and an animal sacrifice, a skinned bloody chicken.

Mr. Sun signals Ken to approach the altar. He does. He is handed a ceremonial goblet, which contains a mixture of wine, and the blood of the chicken.

One of Mr. Sun's men seizes Ken's hand. Ken struggles briefly, then lets them take it. The man makes a cut with a dagger. Ken's blood drips into the mixture in the goblet.

Mr. Sun directs Ken to pass beneath an arch of swords. Mr. Sun then reads an oath on paper, and Ken repeats his words.

> KEN (V.O.)
> The ceremony was a simple one, and ancient.

Mr. Sun then takes the paper on which the oath was written, and burns it on the altar.

> KEN (V.O.) (CONT'D)
> I was now responsible to the gods of old. To perform my duties as instructed.

Ken raises his three fingers on his left hand as a binding gesture -- then he drinks from the goblet.

> KEN (V.O.) (CONT'D)
> And with that, I bowed down, pledging my loyalty to my dying day.

Ken bows humble to Mr. Sun, the way a warrior bows before his emperor.

> MR. SUN
> Arise, my son.

> KEN (V.O.)
> Now I was a soldier for a crime syndicate. Just like my grandfather. My father as well, despite being a cop. I couldn't escape my family's fate, no matter what I did. I had a new family now...

> KEN (CONT'D)
> Yes... father.

INT. KEN'S SAFEHOUSE - NIGHT

Ken is staying in a small studio apartment. Through the window can be seen the arches and paper lanterns of Chinatown.

Ken lies flat on his back on a futon, thinking things over.

                    KEN (V.O.)
          I was safe... for the moment. But there was some other
          shit going down that night...

SERIES OF SHOTS

Jimmy and Carmine Malone meet in a large storehouse with members of the Colombian cartel. Suddenly, SKI-MASKED GUNMEN appear and shoot up the meeting.

Carmine wrestles with one of the gunmen. He rips off the mask: Bassim! Bassim kills Carmine. Jimmy runs for his life and manages to escape.

                    KEN (V.O.)
          Apparently the Bazins had had enough of the truce.
          They were ready to go to war.

Jimmy, disheveled, stands before his father Don Gino.

                    JIMMY
          They killed Carmine. They broke the truce.

Don Gino's face is hard. He looks sad... but ready to wreak deadly vengeance.

                    KEN (V.O.)
          They'd also hit two other Malone storehouses. They
          were looking to make it hurt. But the next day, Jimmy
          found out something that made his life -- and mine --
          infinitely more complicated...

EXT. TOMMY'S APARTMENT - AFTERNOON
Jimmy looks at security camera footage.

The footage shows the front door of the apartment complex.

On the footage: Ken Liu walks in.

Jimmy stares, astonished. He runs the video back and forth. Stops on the image.

It's definitely Ken. No doubt about it.

JIMMY

Ken...

Jimmy's face is pained. He looks almost sick.

His cell rings. Display reads "PAUL MALONE".

JIMMY (CONT'D)

Hey Paulie.

PAUL

Mandatory meeting tomorrow at eleven a.m. My house in Studio City.

JIMMY

I'll be there.

INT. KEN'S SAFEHOUSE - DAY

Ken's cell phone rings. He answers.

KEN

Hello?

JOHNNY (V.O.)

Hey Ken, it's Johnny. Mr. Sun called about an emergency meeting. Jimmy Malone will contact you and give you more details.

                         KEN
What's going on?

                     JOHNNY (V.O.)
        Texting you the meeting info. Don't be late.

EXT. GREEN HILLS CEMETERY - DAY
The morning light slants across the graves. Maggie's is in there somewhere.
That's probably what Ken's thinking as he stares out at them.

    Ken turns, and there's Jimmy. Jimmy tries hard to mask the rage within him.

                         JIMMY
        Ken.

Ken turns around.

                         KEN
        Hey, Jimmy.

Jimmy gestures to a nearby limo.

INT. LIMOUSINE - DAY
Once inside, Ken turns to find himself looking down the barrel of Jimmy's gun.

                         JIMMY
        I should fucking kill you right now.

Ken opens his mouth.

                    JIMMY (CONT'D)
        Don't even try to deny it. I know.

Ken accepts the inevitable.

KEN

I got justice for her. You'd've done the same damn thing.

Jimmy stares back, hateful.

KEN (CONT'D)

My heart's at peace, Jimmy. Do what you gotta do. If you're gonna kill me, get it over with.

Jimmy squeezes the trigger --
    -- can't do it. He lowers the gun. Breathes deeply.

JIMMY

Listen. Here's the thing -- with Tommy dead, our families' alliance is mended.

KEN

What do you mean?

JIMMY

Tommy fucked us too. When he killed Mr. Sun's daughter, he put the entire organization at risk.

Ken nods.

JIMMY (CONT'D)

So the slate's clean. And that's as far as it goes. This shit wouldn't look good to out other contacts.
                    (beat)
We heard you got tipped off.

                              KEN
Who was the informant?

                             JIMMY
I don't know. Word travels fast in our business... but
sometimes it's just rumors. At first my father was
pissed about it. But then he let it go. -- you're okay in
his book.
                            (beat)
I, however, am not your biggest fan.

                              KEN
Sorry to hear that. I really am. I thought you were my
friend.

                             JIMMY
Friends don't go killing other friends' brothers. No
matter how much the son of a bitch deserved it.

Jimmy looks out the window. He shrugs.

                        JIMMY (CONT'D)
Anyway, nobody else seems to give a shit, and there's
peace with Zao. You're under his protection. So I
couldn't touch you even if I wanted to.

                              KEN
                           (annoyed)
Then quit complaining, and let's just go to this thing
and get it over with.

Jimmy stares at Ken. Shakes his head with a little smile. What a ball buster.
    Jimmy knocks on the glass divider. The limo starts moving.

EXT. LIMOUSINE - DAY

The limo winds through the hills of Studio City.

KEN

Where we going?

JIMMY (O.S.)

To my cousin Paul's house. He's the capo in our family. The guy is great with numbers and makes us a lot of scratch.

EXT. PAUL MALONE'S HOUSE - DAY

The limo parks in front of Paul Malone's house and the boys get out. They cross to the front door and Jimmy rings the bell.

PAUL (V.O.)

Who is it?

A camera stares down above the door. Jimmy looks up at it.

JIMMY

It's Jimmy and Ken. Paulie, open up the door, man.

PAUL MALONE, 30s, bearded, good-looking -- a good-natured and serious man -- opens his door to invite the two in. Paul and Jimmy hug warmly.

PAUL

Hey Jimmy, it's good to see you.

JIMMY

Same here, cuz. You look great, man. How do you feel?

PAUL

I'm feeling good, man, feeling good. My girl just gave birth to my first kid, a beautiful little boy.

JIMMY

Good for you! Next time I see you three, I'll christen the little bastard.

PAUL

Hey, fuck you!

They laugh, knowing it's all a joke.

JIMMY

Seriously, I'm happy for you. Congratulations.

PAUL

Thanks. I tell you there's nothing like a bunch of crazy shit-kicking business to bring a family together.

JIMMY

That's funny man. You should be a fucking comedian.

PAUL
(chuckles)

I just might.

JIMMY

Where's my old man?

PAUL

Living room. With the others.
(to Ken)

Ken Liu, right?

Paul and Ken shake.

> KEN
>
> Yeah that's me. Pleasure to meet you.

> PAUL
>
> Paul Malone. This way.

He gestures, and Ken and Jimmy move before him into the living room.

INT. PAUL'S HOUSE - LIVING ROOM - DAY

Seated on antique couches and fancy chairs are top members of the Suns, the Malones, the Russians, the Yakuza, the Mexicans, and Westside Syndicate. Mike Lee is there too. He nods at Ken.

The men are all dressed in business suits, nice plain silk ties, with nice dress shoes and slacks.

> KEN (V.O.)
>
> It looked like the mob United Nations. Guys from the Suns, the Malones, the Russians... the Yakuza, the Mexican Mafia, and the Westside Syndicate. These were the big dogs of L.A. crime, Inc. It made my skin crawl just being in there.

Ken looks up, and Don Gino's coming toward him. Face tight. He know everything. But nothing will be discussed in front of the others.

> DON GINO
>
> Ken, good to see you.
> (sotto)
> Our recent unpleasantness is a thing of the past. Tommy was a menace to the entire organization.

Don Gino goes extremely terse.

> ### DON GINO (CONT'D)
> But you know full well the seriousness of your actions. To threaten my family is an act of war, but given the circumstances, it was justified.

Ken sighs with relief.

> ### DON GINO
> (to the others)
> Gentlemen... let's gets started.

The bosses all sit down. Their henchmen remain standing behind their respective bosses. Jimmy and Ken wait, front and center, like defendants before a panel of judges.

Mr. Sun takes the floor.

> ### MR. SUN
> Ken, you and James here are needed to take care of a problem that is troubling all of our organizations.

> ### KEN
> What is it?

> ### PAUL
> The Bazins have broken the truce and attacked our warehouses. They killed Carmine. They are stealing our suppliers from Columbia and Mexico right and left, and killing anyone who gets in the way.

> ### MR. SUN
> Jimmy was there when it happened and ID'd Bassim Bazin. Son of Asim Bazin. We need you two to find them and kill them.

JIMMY

No outside help?

DON GINO

These pieces of work need to know fear. They want to fuck with us, then they are going to die by us.

MR. SUN

Ken... you should know. Our entire alliance is bound by intermarriage. Everyone in this room is part of the same family. The Bazins do not share our vision, and that makes them enemies.

Ken turns to Don Gino.

DON GINO

I had a dream once of a united organization, one great family with combined efforts in every business endeavor to be found. An international powerhouse, where we could stop the bloodshed and share our combined fortunes. To put it simply, total control over all organized crime all over the world.
(Beat)

KEN

How long has this been going on?

DON GINO

The whole thing started about eight years ago. That is why all of our families intermarried. Your extended family and mine. It worked out well. It made us beyond wealthy. How did you think we acquired the life styles we have? Working nine to five jobs? Not a chance.

Don Gino takes a sip of whiskey.

                    KEN

        I'm impressed.

                  DON GINO

        It was a good dream, a long time ago. Now, it seems,
        that it's under attack.

                   MR. SUN

        You'll need a team on this operation. Do you accept
        the contract?

Ken looks at Jimmy. Jimmy nods. Ken stares back at Mr. Sun... and at Don Gino.

                 KEN (V.O.)
        And that's when I made the dumbest move of my life.

Ken nods.

               KEN (CONT'D)
        I accept.

                   MR. SUN
        Excellent.

Don Gino indicates the other gang leaders and entourage.

                  DON GINO

        Everyone is here to witness this because they honor the
        alliance and support our cause. Mr. Lee will provide
        the logistics and arms for the operation.

He looks over at Mike, who nods obediently.

> DON GINO (CONT'D)
> We all agree --this operation must be done, in the spirit
> of cooperation and mutual respect. No egos, no back
> stabbing and no fuck ups.

Don Gino stands up and approaches the men. He speaks quietly.

> DON GINO (CONT'D)
> As for the matter of any past grievances you two have be-
> tween each other -- better leave that shit behind. Capisci?

Ken and Jimmy look at each other. They'd like to shoot each other right now.
Don Gino lightly slaps each of them, and they look at him.

> DON GINO (CONT'D)
> I said, capisci?

> JIMMY
> Yes.

> KEN
> Yes sir.

> DON GINO
> Good. These are perilous times for the entire fam-
> ily. The last thing we need's some half-assed vendetta
> fucking up the bigger picture.
> (to Paul)
> Paulie, show these gentlemen out.

INT. ZAN & TAI'S SAFE HOUSE - DAY

Zan opens the door for Ken and Jimmy. The afternoon light filters in to the
well-kept domicile.

                    ZAN
Welcome to your new safe house, gentlemen.
                  (to Tai)
Tai?

                    TAI
      This way, boys.

INT. SAFE HOUSE OFFICE - DAY
The lights go on. The place is practically an arms warehouse stocked with weapons and heavy fire power all over the place. Mike Lee is reclining on a sofa against the wall.

                    TAI
      Welcome to Valhalla.

Jimmy and Ken are impressed.

SERIES OF SHOTS
Tai pulls out a footlocker. Unlocks a combination.
      On the table -- Tai slaps down a couple of Uzis.
      Some gleaming M16s.
      A couple of Beretta M9s.
      Some Sig Sauer P226s.
      The ever-reliable AK-47.

BACK TO SCENE

                   JIMMY
      It all looks so tempting.

He begins to cock and prime the guns.

ZAN

And at fair deal to I might add. It's amazing what you can get in this town, just got to know the right people.

KEN

Are you sure this is all necessary? Seems like overkill.

JIMMY

No amount of kill is too much when you're dealing with Bazins.

Jimmy sights with the AK. CLICK.

MIKE

You'll have everything you'll need to get the job done. I know the Bazins' house inside out.

While Jimmy works with his AK, Ken sits down next to Mike.

MIKE (CONT'D)

Something wrong?

KEN

All this time, everyone I know, at least everyone I thought I knew...are you ALL killers?

MIKE

Only when we really need to be. Might seem like a lot to take in, but you made the deal in front of everyone.

Mike gets up and stretches his limbs.

> KEN

Where are you going?

> MIKE

Back to the office. I'm still a lawyer and I still have a
job to do. Gotta keep up appearances.

Mike pats Ken on the shoulder.

> MIKE (CONT'D)

Don't worry about a thing. You're working with the
best. They'll train you, and they'll take care of you.

EXT. STREET - DAY

Mike drives away, leaving Ken watching for inquisitive eyes as Jimmy stows the weapons trunk in a nondescript Honda. The car sags noticeably when the gear's inside.

The two get in and drive off.

EXT. HANGAR - NIGHT

Jimmy and Ken pull up to an abandoned air hangar in an undisclosed location. Torn to shreds from years of neglect and decay, the moonlight shines through gaps in the roof.

> JIMMY

Leave the stuff in the trunk. That's for Bazin. We got
training weapons here. Just follow me.

The two get out. Ken follows Jimmy into the hangar.

INT. HANGAR - NIGHT

It's dark. Jimmy hits a power switch on the wall and a few dim lights snap on. The hanger itself is mostly bare, with a couple of gun lockers. In one alcove is a room, with a fridge, a bathroom and a couple of beds.

Jimmy nods to the bed.

                    JIMMY
Get some Z's, fucko. Because tomorrow I am going to
kick your ass like you never seen.

                    KEN
Do you have to break my balls?

                    JIMMY
I don't have to. It's my pleasure. Good night, fucker.

Jimmy chuckles. Ken lies down. He shakes his head.

                    KEN
Sweet dreams, assface.

              KEN (V.O.) (CONT'D)
I was still kind of afraid he'd kill me if I turned my
back. Sleep was hard to come by that night. I was surprised when I woke up alive.

EXT. HANGAR - DAY
Jimmy leads Ken to an outdoor shooting range on the old cracked runway.
     Zan, Tai and Benny have also arrived, and stand around eating donuts and
drinking coffee.

EXT. SHOOTING RANGE - DAY
Jimmy stands with hands on hips and addresses Ken.

                    JIMMY
You were a quick study with the pistols... but this...
                 (holds up Uzi)
...is another animal entirely.

Ken regards the gun in Jimmy's hands.

> JIMMY (CONT'D)
> Welcome the automatics 101. This is the Uzi, world's
> most popular submachine gun. Weapon of choice for
> insurgents and drug runners everywhere.

> KEN
> Cool.

> JIMMY
> Pull back the top slider to load the gun. Push this little
> button on the back of the weapon to unload the clip --
> push a new clip in underneath the handle chamber -- and
> you're ready for action. Got it?

Jimmy hands the Uzi to Ken. Ken loads the clip into the gun and pulls the slider
back.

> KEN
> Got it.

> JIMMY
> Good. Squeeze off a few shots at that target line with
> the cardboard cut outs.

Ken aims the Uzi and fires at the cardboard target, shooting the head clean off.

> JIMMY (CONT'D)
> Good shot. I'm impressed.

> KEN
> I'm a fast learner.

JIMMY

You got lucky. Don't get a big head wise ass. We're not
done yet.

Benny comes in and joins Jimmy and Ken. Jimmy picks up a sniper rifle and
hands it to Ken.

He shows Ken how to load it. Then attaches a suppressor.

JIMMY (CONT'D)

So we now know -- you can shoot with machine guns.
But if you're gonna be a top dog in this business, you
need to know how to snipe. And snipe well.

KEN

How hard can it be? Where's the target?

Jimmy snickers, he points out to Ken a target in the distance. Ken can hardly
see it.

JIMMY

Five hundred yards out. Think you can hit that,
hotshot?

Ken's mouth drops open.

KEN

Uh...

JIMMY
(laughs)

Benny, show him.

Jimmy hands Benny the sniper rifle.

Benny looks through the scope at the far target -- then takes off the scope.

KEN

Oh, now you're just fuckin' with me. Hey, how come your not using a scope?

BENNY

Using scopes makes your eyes lazy. You got to aim with your soul. Feel the trigger and let your mind do the rest. That subconscious shit.

KEN
(chuckles)

Okay, Yoda.

BENNY
(joking sarcastically)

My ass, you must kiss.

On the word "kiss", Benny fires.
    Hits the target clean.

KEN

Damn.

BENNY

Best sniper in town.

Benny smiles. He reloads the rifle and gives it to Ken. Ken aims and fires but misses.
    Benny smirks. Ken tries again. Misses.

KEN

Shit.

                    BENNY
Give it time. Focus.

                    KEN
Shut up. I got it.

Ken focuses. Struggles to see and line up the target without a scope. He fires
and misses.

                KEN (CONT'D)
Damn it!

                    JIMMY
Better stick with the scope for now. Stay calm when
you fire. You'll get better, you just need more practice.

                    KEN
Yeah. Thanks.

                    JIMMY
Yeah, yeah. Don't think I'm going soft on you. I just
want to make sure you don't end up getting me killed
on this job.
                (to Benny)
Benny? I need a moment alone.

Benny leaves.

                    KEN
I gotta ask you something.

                    JIMMY
Shoot.

KEN

How many people have you... you know... killed?

JIMMY

Thirty.

KEN

Women and kids?

JIMMY

No kids.
(beat)
Women... well... I don't want to talk about it.

KEN

Come on.

Jimmy sighs. Looks off into the distance. Looks back at Ken.

JIMMY

A couple of stupid broads who worked for the family stole from us.
(shrugs)
So, I killed them.

KEN

Damn. That's Cold-hearted.

JIMMY

It's a bitch. But I get the job done. Always.
(beat)
Just remember this -- when we go in there and do this job, don't hesitate to pull the trigger. If you do, we're dead. We don't know how many are there. Don't think -- just shoot.

                    KEN

Is it worth it? All this I mean?

                    JIMMY

Maybe. Maybe not. But this is what we do. It's who we
are. Once you're in, there's no getting out.

                    KEN

Yeah...

                    (debates with himself)

Look, Jimmy... I'm sorry about your brother. I wish it...
I wish...

                    JIMMY

I know. But that don't change things between us. We
both lost people we loved. It's a double-edged sword,
and we both got fuckin' cut. Face it, this business sucks.

Jimmy shakes it off.

                JIMMY (CONT'D)

Tell you what, Hundred bucks says I kick your ass on
the range.

                    KEN

Two hundred and you're on.

The two unlikely allies shake hands.

SERIES OF SHOTS
Jimmy and Ken use pistols and shoot at paper targets. Jimmy shoots eyes and
a mouth on his. He grins at Ken. Ken smiles -- then shoots two testicles and a
three-shot penis on it.
    Benny, Zan and Tai are watching them -- cheering.

> KEN (CONT'D)
>
> Oh, wait...

He adds another shot to the penis, making it longer.

> KEN (CONT'D)
>
> There, that's about right.

Jimmy gives him a sour expression.

Zan and Tai laugh at him.

Jimmy fires his AK. Shreds a target. Ken gives his a try. Cuts the head in half vertically -- as the AK rides up on him. Jimmy shakes his head in disgust.

Back to pistols. Jimmy hits the center of his target. Ken hits the center of his. Jimmy pops one in the head. Ken matches on his. He grins over at Jimmy, who frowns.

An empty Sparkletts bottle explodes. In the distance, Jimmy lowers the sniper rifle. Looks over at Ken with a "how ya like me now?" look.

Another empty Sparkletts bottle remains whole. A slug hits the dirt. A slug hits a rock. Then -- CRASH! In the distance, Ken throws up his arm in triumph. Jimmy high fives it.

Ken fires the AK. He's got it under control now. He shreds one, two, three targets. Jimmy nods, grudgingly impressed.

The two fire a full clip each. They get their targets and look at each other's strangely. They overlay them. The holes are almost identical.

EXT. SHOOTING RANGE - LATER

Jimmy and Ken face off.

> JIMMY
>
> Not bad.

> KEN
>
> Not bad at all.

                          JIMMY
A draw then.

                           KEN
A draw.

                          JIMMY
Now it's time for the real deal. And no paper targets.
But trust me -- it'll be a real blast.

EXT. SHERMAN OAKS MANSION - DAY
It's just after noon. A black SUV with tinted windows drives up the quiet street.
And parks in the driveway of the mansion next door to the Bazins.

EXT. SUV - DAY
The engine cuts.

                        ZAN (O.S.)
We're gonna smoke those motherfuckers. Gangsta-style.

                        TAI (O.S.)
Fuckin' A! I haven't had a hit squad like this for a long
time.

                        PAUL (O.S.)
Okay, gents. Remember Scarface? When Sosa's men
floored Tony Montana's place? Just like that, only this
is for real.

INT. SUV - DAY
Ken, Jimmy, Benny, Paul, Zan and Tai sit inside.
    All wear trench coats with dress shirts and ties, black dress pants, dress
shoes, dark sunglasses and ski masks. Bulk under the dress shirts indicates
they're all vested.

Each fits a communication headset.

> JIMMY
>
> Okay. You all know the layout. They've got about forty guards around the place. Benny will go up high and snipe -- he'll be our eyes. Once we get the lay of the land we'll split up and do the deed.

Jimmy and Paul are armed with M16s with suppressors. Ken is armed with an Uzi, with suppressor. Zan and Tai are armed with AK-47s. Benny has a Sniper rifle with a suppressor and radio.

> JIMMY (CONT'D)
>
> Any questions? No? Anybody have to go the bath-room? No?

The guys laugh, Ken somewhat nervously.

> JIMMY (CONT'D)
>
> Alright, boys. Remember where we parked.

EXT. SUV - DAY

The hit squad exits the SUV. Zan and Tai carry bags. They sneak through the bushes and up the driveway of the Bazin house toward the back.

EXT. BAZIN BACKYARD - DAY

A group of six henchmen armed with pistols, AK-47s, and shotguns stand guard around Bassim, who sits in a lounge chair on the deck around the Olympic-sized pool.

Bassim, handsome and fit, wears only a pair of black swim trunks. Expensive shades hide his eyes.

There are various sexy bikini girls chilling around the pool with drinks. But the action is on the meeting Bassim is having, with Deja at his side.

His opposite number is MIGUEL REBENGA, 30s, flanked by two body-guards. Rebenga doesn't seem relaxed or comfortable. Which of course is Bassim's intention.

> BASSIM
>
> You know we got hard core connections. Right? Al Qaeda in Afghanistan. All it takes is a word from me, and I'll have a suitcase dirty bomb in the trunk of a car, that's parked in front of your fuckin' house in Colombia. Think about that when you're thinking about stiffing me, my friend.

Deja, wearing expensive Prada sunglasses, and busty in a purple bikini, laughs and looks off in a bored way.

Bassim shoots her a glance. Rebenga does too -- he likes those boobs.

INT. EMPTY HOUSE - DAY

Benny moves through a vacant house, to a 2nd floor window overlooking the Bazin backyard. He hunkers down and pulls out binocs.

EXT. DRIVEWAY - DAY

The kill team waits in the bushes.

> BENNY (V.O.)
>
> Bassim and Deja. They're meeting with the Colombians.

EXT. BAZIN BACKYARD - DAY

Bassim stares insolently at Rebenga.

> REBENGA
>
> What we give you, is what you get.

BASSIM

What I <u>want</u> is twenty-five. Ten million was not the deal. Stick to the arrangement you made... unless you want to glow in the dark.

REBENGA

Fuck you.

BASSIM

No, fuck you! We do business my way -- or no deal!

REBENGA

Alright, alright. Fine.
(smiles)
Just trying to haggle. That's business, right? It's just business.

Bassim just stares at him. Rebenga's not winning this guy over at all.

REBENGA (CONT'D)

We'll give you the shipping ASAP. I'll call my suppliers.

BASSIM

Good. Prepare the shipment to leave tomorrow night. Understand?

REBENGA

Whatever you say, Mr. Bazin.

BASSIM

Excellent. My men'll meet you tomorrow evening to make the exchange.
(totally insincere)
Pleasure doing business with you.

Rebenga and his men leave. With a lingering glance at Deja.
When they're gone, she shudders.

> DEJA
> Ugh, I feel like I need a shower.

> BASSIM
> That little cock sucker.

> DEJA
> What's your problem? You totally scared the shit out
> of him.

> BASSIM
This asshole nearly ruined the deal. I would have lost it if I didn't have Mr.
Blanco working for our business... Deja, remind me to thank him for the last job
he did for us.

> DEJA
> Yes, he can clean house well, can't he? It's a good thing
> that I hired him to work for us.

> BASSIM
> Good thing. I'm sick of this bullshit.

> DEJA
> Bassim. Fuckin' chill out. Stop worrying so much.
> Soon enough, we'll own this town.

She proffers her drink for him to toast.

> DEJA (CONT'D)
> Just take it easy, baby. Think good thoughts.

Bassim brings his own drink up. He toasts and drains his drink.

> BASSIM
>
> Hey, butler! Another one!

Bassim's butler quickly hightails it to pool side with a fresh drink. Then, TRIPS -- and spills it all over Bassim!

> BASSIM (CONT'D)
>
> What the fuck! You stupid asshole!

The butler quivers in fear.

> BUTLER
>
> I'm sorry Mr. Bazin! Forgive me!

The butler is seized by Bassim's bodyguards.

> BASSIM
>
> Hey, settle down, buddy. It's no problem.

Without warning, Bassim shoots him with a silenced pistol. In the leg. The butler screams, but a bodyguard's got a hand around his mouth. The chicks in the deep end look over blandly, then turn back to their animated conversation. Bassim, with a look of distaste, hooks a thumb. The bodyguards haul the guy off. He can still be heard gurgling and moaning -- but TWO SILENCED GUNSHOTS put a stop to that.

> DEJA
>
> Jesus, you could have just fired the guy.

> BASSIM
>
> I just did.

EXT. EMPTY HOUSE - DAY
Benny has witnessed everything.

> BENNY
> (into radio)
> Bassim just had his butler killed because the poor bas-
> tard spilled a drink.

> PAUL (V.O.)
> This guy will be a pleasure to kill.

EXT. DRIVEWAY - DAY
Jimmy nods.

> JIMMY
> Then let's get to it. Ken, Zan, Tai -- mansion. Let's party.

Jimmy and Paul open the gate and slip through while Ken, Zan and Tai head for the front door.

Jimmy and Paul open fire. The guards are totally taken by surprise. Jimmy and Paul drop them methodically. The bikini girls around the pool start screaming.

Benny, from his vantage point above, snipes guards here and there.

Deja and Bassim overturn the picnic table and scramble behind it for cover.

INT. SHERMAN OAKS MANSION - DAY
The door blows off its hinges. Guards look up. Some are playing a video game, others are eating relaxedly.

They all die. A flatscreen with Call of Duty on it is shot to pieces, just as animated soldiers come in firing rifles at the player's character.

Guards reach for their guns, but it's too late -- and Zan, Ken and Tai are too quick. The bodies pile up.

EXT. BAZIN BACKYARD - DAY

The carnage continues. The air fills with smoke. Moving sideways, Jimmy and Paul mow down the remaining guards. Bikini girls freak and run into the line of fire. A particularly hot one gets shot.

                         JIMMY
          Damn.

                         PAUL
          Look out!

He shoves Jimmy to the ground as bullets pierce the air where his head was. Deja and Bassim are armed and return fire.

     Paul whips a burst of covering fire. Deja and Bassim take a chance and sprint for the cover of some cabanas. Paul takes this lull to assess Jimmy's condition.

                         JIMMY
          I'm fine. You saved my life.

                         PAUL
          What are cousins for?

INT. SHERMAN OAKS MANSION - DAY

Ken, Zan and Tai step over dead guard bodies as they plant explosives in key areas of the mansion.

                         KEN
                     (into radio)
          Is Asim back there?

                         PAUL (V.O.)
          No, just the kids.

Gunfire is heard on the line and in the air.

                              KEN
                          (into radio)
                   I'm coming out there!

                          PAUL (V.O.)
                   Negative, find Asim!

Ken beckons to Zan and Tai. They run upstairs.

EXT. BAZIN BACKYARD - DAY
Paul and Jimmy are covering on the other side of the table where Deja and
Bassim were. Deja and Bassim are taking potshots from the cabanas.

                             JIMMY
              This is bullshit. An RPG would end this right now.

                             PAUL
                   Suck it up. Wait till they reload.

They take the opportunity to reload themselves.

INT. SHERMAN OAKS MANSION - DAY
Guards pop out of bedrooms, fully alerted and firing like crazy. Ken, Zan and
Tai duck into rooms themselves, pop in and out.
      The fat guards are just not quick enough. The three work their way toward
the end of the hall -- master bedroom.

EXT. BAZIN BACKYARD - DAY
A sudden silence from the cabanas.

                             PAUL
                   It's now or never.

They run flat out, firing all the way.

Jimmy's gun jams. He hurls it aside and pulls out his pistol.
Bassim pops out, fires -- Jimmy ducks, returns fire, hits Bassim in the arm.

BASSIM

Aw, shit!

He drops his weapon and drops to the ground, screaming.

DEJA (O.S.)

Bassim!

She pulls him by the leg into the cabana.
Jimmy and Paul stand there, shooting up the cabana. It's surprisingly strong.

PAUL

Fuck, it's a panic room!

Deja can be heard laughing inside.

INT. SHERMAN OAKS MANSION - DAY
Ken, Zan and Tai bust open the master bedroom door.
Empty. Zan ducks into the bathroom.

ZAN

It's empty. He ain't here.

Gunshots ring out from below. And a new sound...
SIRENS.

EXT. BAZIN BACKYARD - DAY
Paul gestures to Jimmy. He's got an idea. They speak overly loudly.

PAUL

Hey, put those explosives on there. No way they'll stand up to all that C4!

JIMMY

You got it!

DEJA (O.S.)

Wait!

JIMMY

Fuck you!

DEJA (O.S.)

Listen! We got money. A lot of money. We can make a deal.

Ken, Zan and Tai, running low, join Jimmy and Paul.

DEJA (O.S.) (CONT'D)

Cease fire, okay? Let's talk business.

INT. CABANA - DAY

Deja smiles. She cocks her pistol. Bassim, bleeding freely, cocks his as well.

DEJA

You take the one on the left, I'll take the one on the right. In the head, just like the Daddy showed us.

Bassim nods.

JIMMY (O.S.)

Sure, okay. Talk.

EXT. BAZIN BACKYARD - DAY

Jimmy motions Ken, Zan and Tai to flanking positions. They move aside.

> JIMMY
>
> I'm putting down my gun. Come on out. Hands where
> I can see 'em.

Deja pokes her head out. She smiles pretty.

> DEJA
>
> Hey, sexy.

She steps outside, holding her hands in the air. Bassim follows her, same deal.

Ken, however, on the side, can see -- each has a gun jammed in the crack of their ass.

> KEN
>
> They're packing!
>
> (to the pair)
>
> Freeze, motherfuckers!

Deja turns, sees Ken standing there. She reaches for her gun -- never makes it. Ken shoots her in the left shoulder.

Bassim sees his sister fall, reaches for his gun.

> BASSIM
>
> You bast--

Jimmy and Paul turn him into dogfood.

The guns fall silent. Sirens can be heard clearly.

BENNY (V.O.)
Cops! Down the hill, comin' up fast!

PAUL
Time to boogie, boys. Ken, move now!

Deja, still alive, hears the name. She tracks Ken running out. Then passes out.

INT. VACANT HOUSE - DAY
Benny vacates his position.

BENNY
(into radio)
Back to the car! Come on!

EXT. DRIVEWAY - DAY
The team bursts out of the backyard.

JIMMY
You get Asim?

ZAN
He wasn't here.

JIMMY
Something's not right...

Together they crash through the foliage to the SUV.

The sirens are louder. But instead of cops, a utility van bursts through the hedges and across the yard toward them.

It's a group of SKI-MASKED killers, just like the ones at the robbery and the sabotage.

The van brakes and they jump out, firing.

The hit squad returns fire and takes cover behind the SUV. Which is quickly bullet holed, tires shot out.

Tai and Zan roll grenades under the car and toward the masked killers.

The masked killers run for their lives -- explosions blow one of them through the front window of the vacant house.

Benny comes upon the scene. He can't figure out what the hell's going on.

                    JIMMY (CONT'D)
                       (to Benny)
          Come on!

They run around the destroyed SUV and pile into the masked killers' van. As police lights appear down the block, the hit squad peels out in the other direction.

INT. VAN - DAY
The hit squad is amped. Benny drives them frantically away from the scene.

                    JIMMY
          What the fuck was that?

                    TAI
          Who the hell were those guys?

                    PAUL
          Where was the fuck was Asim!

                    ZAN
          He wasn't there!

                    JIMMY
          Well we were told he would be! Now we're in shit deep-
          er than we can climb out of.

(to Ken)
This is all your fuckin' fault.

KEN

Fuck you!

JIMMY

Fuck you!

BENNY

Uh, boys...

JIMMY
(to Benny)
We got to think of something quick, or we're dead.

BENNY

We've got company.

Benny points out the back. Black cars are following them. Bazin guys lean out, firing Uzis.

Benny zigs and zags across the road, trying to outmaneuver them.

Behind the Bazins -- the cops.

Benny turns wildly onto a freeway onramp.

EXT. FREEWAY - DAY
Bazins and cops trail the van across the freeway lanes. Overhead a helicopter joins the chase.

ZAN (O.S.)
We are in a world of shit.

INT. VAN - DAY
The hit squad finds a tear gas gun and an M16.

TAI

Well, least we're not without means.

They quick set up the M16, pointing out the back.

JIMMY

Me and Paul will watch the flanks. Just keep shooting
until no bad guys are left.

Paul and Jimmy take up positions in the side windows and start firing.

Ken nods to Tai and Zan -- who throw open the back doors.

Ken opens fire.

EXT. FREEWAY - DAY

A Bazin riding on the passenger door is the first recipient of the M16'S lead. He
goes flying -- a Toyota runs him over.

Ken rakes the other cars. They fall back. One driver gets it in the head, and
his car goes over the center divider into oncoming traffic. It flips over and over
-- the destruction is epic.

The Bazins are all gone -- then bullets pierce the roof!

A cop with an M16 is leaning out the helicopter door, firing!

INT. VAN - DAY

The boys roll to the sides as Paul and Jimmy open fire on the helicopter.
Tai hands the tear gas gun to Ken.

TAI

Make him cry.

Ken hangs out the back of the van, inches from the speeding freeway. He whips
out the tear gas gun, and one-handed, takes a bead.

EXT. FREEWAY - DAY

The helicopter pilot swerves away, presenting the open window -- Ken scores a hole in one!

The cockpit instantly fills with gas.

A news chopper has joined the chase -- the police copter swings out and rams it. Both choppers fall down into the suburban foliage below.

INT. VAN - DAY

Tai and Zan pull Ken in and shut the doors.

EXT. THE FREEWAY - DAY

The van hits an offramp heading to South L.A.

Too late Benny sees there's a spike strip in his way.

> BENNY
>
> Hold on!

Benny plows through the strip, shredding the tires!

He fights to keep control.

The van blows through the roadblock, and cops fire after it.

The van crashes through a chain-link fence and into the wash below!

Miraculously, Benny keeps the van upright.

> BENNY (CONT'D)
>
> Fuckin' shit!

> JIMMY
> (points)
>
> There!

A giant sewer pipe yawns before them. Benny fishtails right into the pipe and they drive up it and out of sight.

EXT. SHERMAN OAKS MANSION - LATER
Bazin soldiers disarm the bombs and gather their dead. Deja is alive but wounded.

> DEJA
> (into phone)
> Father, they attacked us!

INT. ACCESS CUSTOM JET - DAY
Asim, enraged, clutches his cellphone with white-knuckled hands.

> DEJA (V.O.)
> They shot up everything. They killed most of our
> guards. And they killed Bassim!

> ASIM
> That's it then. If it's war they want, then Hell shall
> open its mouth for them.

Asim hangs up. He turns his attention to his informant.

> ASIM (CONT'D)
> Thanks you for providing me the information. You
> shall be rewarded.

The informant reveals himself: Mike Lee.

INT. HOSPITAL - LATER
Deja is bandaged and IV'ed. A nurse fusses over her.

> DEJA
> Jesus, give me a moment's peace! Get the fuck out!

The nurse, pissed, exits. Deja whips out her cell and dials a number. She listens.

DEJA (CONT'D)
Rico. I need you to find Ken Liu and his men. And
don't miss this time, like you did outside Tommy's.

INT. RICO'S APARTMENT - DAY
RICO BLANCO, 40s, Colombian cleaner, looks pissed. Dangerous.

RICO
I won't.

DEJA (V.O.)
Better not, you fuckup. In fact... I'm coming with.

Rico gets his weapons squared away.

INT. HOSPITAL - LATER
Deja smiles.

DEJA
I want that bastard myself. Get their location and call
me back.

Deja hangs up. Asim enters. She puts on the daddy's little girl act. He kisses her
forehead.

ASIM
How are you, my darling?

DEJA
(pouts)
It hurts, Daddy.

INT. BUS - DAY (BACK TO PRESENT)
Ken, dressed unobtrusively in tourist wear, sunglasses and bucket hat, tries to blend in.

> KEN (V.O.)
> It was a difficult time. Even though I had powerful friends... I was still on the run. In this business, you can spend a lot of time on the run. Now I know how my father felt...

FLASHBACK - INT. SAFEHOUSE - DAY
One by one, the boys enter. They're wasted and beat. Tai and Zan flop on the couch. Paul peeks through a gap in the windowshade.
    Ken enters -- Jimmy points down the hall. Ken disappears into the hallway. Jimmy pulls out his cell -- decides he can't handle it at the moment -- sits down with Zan and Tai.
    Benny hits the fridge, gets beers. Tosses them to each. They crack the beers. Drink. Each thinking their thoughts.

INT. SAFEHOUSE BATHROOM - DAY
Ken sits on the can. Dials a number. The YAMMER of voice mail comes on the line. And a BEEP.

> KEN
> Hung, it's Ken. Listen... you and your parents have to get the hell out of town. Don't ask why, just do it.

He hangs up. Thinks. Dials another number.

> FEMALE VOICE (V.O.)
> You have one new message. Press--

Ken dials in the code.

HUNG (V.O.)

Ken, listen to me! My parents were murdered in their home! I just found out! Goddamn you, Ken! I told you not to get involved with those people! I've lost my whole family thanks to you!

Ken hangs up, looking spooked. And guilty as hell.

INT. SAFEHOUSE - DAY

Jimmy drinks, closes his eyes. He rubs his temples.

His phone rings. He looks at the display, then at Paul. Paul looks grim.

JIMMY

Hello?

INT. DON MALONE'S HOUSE - LIVING ROOM - DAY

Don Malone sits before a newscast showing "BREAKING NEWS" on the shootout.

DON GINO

You fucking assholes! Have you seen the news?! Every fucking news station in town is broadcasting what happened.

JIMMY (V.O.)

We couldn't find Asim. It was an ambush. It's not our fault.

DON GINO

I don't give a shit whose fault it was! This was supposed to be done discreetly, and you've brought everything out into the open! Soon the Feds will be hunting us down!

INT. SAFEHOUSE - DAY

Paul grimaces at the loud sound of Don Gino's voice.

                    DON GINO (V.O.)
          Where the hell are you?!

                    JIMMY
          At the safe house, laying low until the heat cools down.
          We barely got out with our fuckin' lives.

                    DON GINO (V.O.)
          Thank God for that.   Listen, the police are already
          starting their investigation.

                    JIMMY
          What are they saying on the news?

                    DON GINO (V.O.)
          Just a bunch of corpses, no live witnesses.

                    JIMMY
          Figures. Pop, don't you see? It was a setup.

INT. DON GINO'S HOUSE - LIVING ROOM - DAY

Don Gino shakes his head.

                    DON GINO
          Impossible. Mike Lee gave us all the information.

                    JIMMY (V.O.)
                    (suspicious)
          So where is he now?

DON GINO

I don't know. But I'll find out.

He sits forward, poking the air like Jimmy's right in front of him.

DON GINO (CONT'D)

Listen, to me -- get out of LA. Head out to the City
of Industry. Meet me at the old Beaumont Warehouse.

EXT. DON GINO'S HOUSE - DAY

Out of sight in a car under a huge tree, Agent Briggs and Agent Ramirez listen
in.

DON GINO (V.O.)

24600 Proctor Avenue.

Ramirez writes down the address. Briggs puts the car in gear and they drive off.

EXT. WAREHOUSE (CITY OF INDUSTRY) - DAY

A shitty warehouse near a large junkyard. Smog sits in noxious layers in the sky.

INT. WAREHOUSE - DAY

Twenty or so armed bodyguards mill about a large warehouse space. Crates, rail-
ings, stairways and catwalks ring the space. Upstairs, an office is tucked into a
corner.

INT. WAREHOUSE OFFICE - DAY

Alex Gomez stands hands on hips. Jimmy, Ken and Don Gino are there.

ALEX

Don't worry, we're here to protect you guys. The
Mexican Mafia's got your back.
(beat)
But you do know you're in a world of shit?

Jimmy just looks at him.

> ALEX (CONT'D)
> I mean, not only did you miss Asim -- Deja's still alive too.

Jimmy shakes his head, irritated at the news.
    While they talk, Ken turns to Don Gino.

> KEN
> Shouldn't we be out there trying to find Mikey?

> DON GINO
> Too much heat. There'll be time for that later.

He looks at Ken, who's clearly unnerved.

> DON GINO (CONT'D)
> Try and relax, alright? You'll live longer. I've been in bad shit before, and look how old I am.

> KEN
> I'm sorry.

> DON GINO
> That's okay. We'll get through this shit. All of us. I called Zao and Johnny ten minutes before I got here, they're looking for Mike too.

> KEN
> How could Mikey do this to us? He was my friend. I trusted him.

> DON GINO

In this business, friends can turn on you just like that. Even the oldest friends you got.

Alex, overhearing this, nods in a commiserating way.

> JIMMY

Pop, we should get the fuck out of dodge. Staying here is too risky.

> DON GINO

Alex has got some of Sergei Dimitri's guys coming to help us. He put in the call a half hour ago.

> KEN

Who?

> JIMMY

Russians.

> ALEX

A truck's on its way. They'll smuggle you out of the city to a safe spot.

EXT. WAREHOUSE - DAY

Tucked away in an alley, with a view of the warehouse, a black van sits.

Rico Blanco watches from within. He looks up the street and sees a truck driving up.

INT. RICO'S VAN - DAY

Rico pulls out a walkie-talkie and thumbs the button.

> RICO

They're here.

ASIM (V.O.)

Good. Kill them.

Rico switches the dial and thumbs the button again.

RICO

Attack team, move in now.

SQUAD COMMANDER (V.O.)

Copy that. Ready to go.

Down the street from the warehouse, an oversized SWAT TEAM truck explodes out. From the side window, an assassin fires a grenade launcher.

The Russians are taken completely by surprise. Their truck explodes in a giant fireball.

INT. WAREHOUSE - DAY

The boys hear the thunder outside.

DON GINO

What the hell?

Without warning, the wooden doors of the warehouse explode inward, and the SWAT TEAM truck careens inside. The violence takes out most of the guards in the truck bay -- the others spin out of harm's way, and pull their guns.

Don Gino, Paul, Jimmy and Ken run out of the upstairs office. From the van, gunmen stream out -- and start firing.

DON GINO (CONT'D)

Behind the pallets!

They dive for the cover of some pallets. Alex, stuck in the office, dives under his desk.

Gunfire splinters the wood, and fragments fill the air. Ken and the Malones shield their eyes and return fire.

One by one, the fake SWAT team goes down in the crossfire. Jimmy lobs a grenade which rolls under the front of the truck and explodes. Fire and shrapnel fill the warehouse, killing the remaining fake SWAT members.

Alex, meanwhile, slips into a trash chute in the wall, and disappears.

In the quiet, the three surviving Malone henchmen walk out to the center of the floor, dazed.

HENCHMAN

What the fuck!

Suddenly, three masked assassins burst through the skylight. They rappel down in a shower of glass, firing. The three henchmen are cut down.

The assassins have not seen the boys upstairs. Don Gino whistles.

They turn around, their eyes wide.

Don Gino and the others open fire, shredding them to pieces. They fall bonelessly to the ground.

More men burst in through the splintered doors, and a fresh round of automatic gunfire echoes in the warehouse.

Before anyone can react, Don Gino is shot. He falls, his gun falling over the railing to the floor below.

The boys return fire, causing a brief lull downstairs.

DON GINO

Get out of here!

JIMMY

No!

The men downstairs regroup and start firing again. Paul is shot and killed. Jimmy and Ken fire back, but they know they only have seconds to live.

DON GINO

Go, goddammit! Go!

Jimmy, torn, yanks Ken away from the edge and toward a window in the back. They now can't be seen from below.

Instead of going out the window, Jimmy grabs a window air conditioning sitting there and hurls it through the window. It makes a loud crash. Then he hauls Ken into a dark corner.

VOICE (O.S.)

They went out the back window! Get 'em!

Then, through the broken door step Rico Blanco and Asim and Deja Bazin. Along with Alex Gomez. Deja's arm is in a sling, still recovering from the bullet wound in her shoulder.

Men grab Don Gino and haul him down the stairs. They stand him before Asim.

Jimmy and Ken find they can see through gaps in the deck -- they can watch the action, unseen.

ASIM

Well, look who we have here. This is a happy surprise.

DON GINO

Gomez, you cocksucker!

ALEX

Hey, if you and the Chinese hadn't teamed up against
the Bazins, none of this would have ever happened.

DON GINO

You backstabbing son of a bitch. You got no honor.

ALEX

Don't hit me with that old world "honor" shit. It's just
business. As for the Bazins -- they line my pockets better than that old alliance shit ever did.

Asim, looking faintly annoyed, holds out a hand.

ASIM

The photos?

Alex hand pictures of Jimmy Malone, Benny Wong, Zan, Tai and Ken Liu to
Asim and Deja.

DEJA

That's them.

(whines)

I want them all.

Asim lights up a small Cuban cigar with his steel lighter and smokes a puff. He
beckons to some operatives. They bring an occupied body bag, and unzip it
before Don Gino.
Mike Lee's corpse.
Ken startles. Jimmy digs his fingers into Ken's shoulder to keep him quiet.

DEJA (CONT'D)

Mike Lee was on our payroll. He served his purpose.
You guys had your time. Now it's our turn.

DON GINO

Cunt.

Rico kicks Don Gino in the guts. Don Gino's losing a lot of blood. And losing
consciousness.

ASIM
(offended)
Language, Mr. Malone. Let's keep this civil.

Asim crouches down before Don Gino.

ASIM (CONT'D)
I do apologize for this raid. Further bloodshed can be
avoided if you simply reveal the whereabouts of the assassins who killed my son.

Don Gino, bleeding freely, is holding on. He rallies, his old toughness flashing
for a moment.

DON GINO
Go fuck yourself, camel jockey. I'll see you in hell.

Asim stands, shakes his head. He motions to Rico.
      Rico pulls out a crowbar and attacks.
      Jimmy and Ken watch the carnage. And cringe at its brutality. Ken looks
away and leaves. But Jimmy forces himself to watch. Etching it into his memory...

EXT. DOWNTOWN LA - NIGHT
Jimmy and Ken drive in a black Honda Accord. Their faces are grim. They don't
speak.

INT. JIMMY'S CAR - NIGHT
Jimmy's stone, Ken's agitated.

KEN
Jimmy, what are we gonna--

JIMMY
Shut up.

Jimmy swerves the car over to the side, pitching Ken across it. Next thing he knows, Jimmy's gun is against his temple.

                    JIMMY (CONT'D)
        Your shit bag friend got my father killed. Far as I'm
        concerned, that's on you.

                         KEN
        That's bullshit, and you know it. Besides, don't you feel
        something poking in your guts?

Jimmy looks down. Ken's gun is right up against his belly.

                    KEN (CONT'D)
        We could kill each other now, like a couple of dick-
        heads. Or, we can stick together, and take down the
        Bazins.

Jimmy shakes his head. Puts his gun away. Sits up, composes himself.

                    KEN (CONT'D)
        I know you're grieving. I know what it's like. I lost my
        parents too. And my baby sister and brother. Nothing
        will bring them back -- nothing'll bring back your fa-
        ther. We take out the Bazins -- then that's justice. And
        you need me.

Jimmy stares at Ken.

                    KEN (CONT'D)
        Who can we go to? Think.

JIMMY

Big Billy Ramon. He might be able to help us if I can
get in touch with him.

KEN

Where is he?

JIMMY

How the fuck should I know? Let's just go meet Mr.
Sun and talk it over.

INT. ELECTRIC ALLEY CLUB - NIGHT

The club's busy. Ken and Jimmy move anonymously through the dim-lit bodies,
all gyrating to the sound of pulsing K-Pop techno.

Various club party girls dance in the club with all types of people. Ravers,
clubbers, civilians, babes in full blown body paint and pasties. Hot go-go girls
dance in cages on stage booths.

Jimmy and Ken walk up the stairs to the office. Zan and Tai step forward
to greet them.

ZAN

Good, you made it. What happened?

Jimmy shakes his head. Zan and Tai see the looks on their faces, and back off.
Tai knocks on the door, listens. He waves them in.

INT. MR. SUN'S OFFICE - NIGHT

Benny stands guard. Mr. Sun sits at his desk, smoking. Johnny leans against the
wall. Jimmy and Ken enter.

MR. SUN

Come and sit down.

They sit.

MR. SUN (CONT'D)
(to Jimmy)
Don Gino was a good man. My condolences.

JIMMY
Thanks.

Mr. Sun stands up and comes around the desk. He moves to the bar and pours himself a glass of sake from a green bottle.

MR. SUN
You two know already that the Bazins have their guys looking us. The remainder of our respective families' factions have gone into hiding.

KEN
Do you know where they took his body?

JOHNNY
No. These guys have covered their tracks too well.

JIMMY
We should have stayed with him, when they hit up the warehouse. Them and fucking Gomez. Traitors.

KEN
He knew he was going to die. If we had stayed, they would have killed us too.

JIMMY
I'm gonna kill everyone of those assholes and rip their fucking heads off.

JOHNNY
What happened to Paul and Mike?

JIMMY
They're dead. Mike was the rat. Lotta good it did him. Alex and the Mexican Mafia are aligned with the Bazins and the Colombians.

KEN
Those weren't ordinary cops -- they were rent-a-cops.

JOHNNY
Dammit. This is more serious than I thought it was going to be.

MR. SUN
All the territories we once controlled in the city have been taken over by the Mexican Mafia and Yakuza. They're all siding with Bazin. The Russians are in hiding.

KEN
So we're low on contacts and resources?

MR. SUN
The rest of the other triads in Chinatown and other Asian gangs in the burbs, who operate independently -- none of them want to get involved. Gutless. So we're on our own.

JIMMY
How did you learn about this?

JOHNNY

Word travels fast around town.

JIMMY

How do we know you guys aren't the ones who set us
up? Maybe you're feeding us a bunch of bullshit!

Jimmy draws his pistol at Mr. Sun and Johnny. Johnny and Ken draw on Jimmy.
Mr. Sun waves them off. Moves toward Jimmy, walking boldly right toward the
barrel of his loaded gun.

MR. SUN

I understand you're upset. Your father requested that I
stay low key in town -- so I did. If I really wanted to have
you and the others killed, James... you'd be dead now.

KEN

Jimmy, Jesus Christ, put the gun down.

Jimmy sighs, puts his gun away.

JIMMY

I'm sorry. It's been a rough day.

Mr. Sun smiles faintly, pats his shoulder.

MR. SUN
(smiles)
Please don't do that again. I'm liable to take offense.

JIMMY

So what's the plan? We can't hide. Sooner or later
they're going to find us. We're all alone here.

MR. SUN

That's right. Which is why we have to go on the offensive. Be proactive about our fates. Top priority -- keep us all alive. And that's what I'm going to do.

Mr. Sun nods at Johnny.

JOHNNY

We do know one thing. A guy named Rico Blanco is helping the Bazins. Through a contact I managed to get a copy of Blanco's criminal file.

Johnny shows a picture.

JIMMY

That's the guy.

KEN

He was there. He's the one who killed Don Gino.

JOHNNY

This guy is dangerous as hell. A former special forces commando type.

JIMMY

We can take him, don't worry about that. I'll gut the fuck like a pig.

MR. SUN

Be careful, still. Both of you.

JOHNNY

The word is that all the major crime families in the city are going to be having a mass gathering in the

next few days. Including the Bazins. If we can find
out where...

> JIMMY

Unleash the wrath of God.

> MR. SUN

That's right. First we need to find out if these rumors
are true or not. If they are, we can start to make plans
for war.

> JOHNNY

But we need allies. The only chance we have to stop
Bazin is to gather up all the independent crews in the
city.

> JIMMY

Big Billy's the man to set that up.

EXT. CHINATOWN - NIGHT

The limo pulls up to the curb. The door opens and Mr. Sun and Ken step out.

> JIMMY

We'll meet you at the safe house after we set up things
with Big Billy.

> MR. SUN

Be careful. Watch your backs.

The door closes and the limo moves off. Mr. Sun rubs his tired eyes.

> KEN

We'll be there in a minute. I think it's safe enough for
you to get some rest.

MR. SUN

Don't ever grow old, Ken. It really sucks.

The two head down the street toward Ken's safehouse.

KEN

Do you really think we'll survive all this?

MR. SUN

War's bad for business. Deep down, nobody really wants it. We manage to get Bazin and his crew, then the others will lose their taste for it. Provided we don't lose our nerve...

Ken looks up to see two figures approaching.

KEN

...and manage to stay out of trouble.

Agent Briggs and Agent Ramirez, smiling, walk up to the two.

AGENT BRIGGS

Too late for that, I'd say.

Agent Ramirez holds a gun on them. Agent Briggs cuffs them both. He begins marching them toward a sedan parked up the street.

AGENT BRIGGS (CONT'D)

Zao Sun. Ken Liu. You're under arrest. You have the right to remain silent.

KEN

Fuck you.

> AGENT BRIGGS

If you give up that right, anything you say can and will
be used against you.

> KEN

Fuck you.

> AGENT BRIGGS

You have the right to an attorney. You can afford one,
so we'll skip the rest of the legal redirect. Do you understand your rights, I've said to you?

They reach the car. Ken catches sight of the man sitting in the back seat, just
inside the open door.

> KEN

Son of a bitch.

Hung steps out of the car, smooths out his suit jacket. He throws down a cigarette and crushes it out.
Without warning, he rams a punch into Ken's solar plexus. Ken falls to his
knees, choking.

> HUNG

You piece of shit. You're dead to me! My parents are
dead because of you. You're a fucking disgrace!

Mr. Sun glares at Hung. Hung turns to him.

> HUNG (CONT'D)

Quit eyeballin' me, you old bastard.
>> (to Agent Briggs)

We done here?

Agent Briggs nods. He and Agent Ramirez put Ken and Mr. Sun in the car, then get in. Hung realizes they're going to strand him here.

                    HUNG (CONT'D)
          Hey. You can't just leave me here!

                    AGENT RAMIREZ
          Call a cab.

The car roars off, leaving Hung standing there fuming.

EXT. PHAT CAT RECORDS - NIGHT
Jimmy, Benny, Zan, Tai and Johnny meet up with The Westside Syndicate representative -- PRIEST, mid 30s, a tall muscular African-American, has a mohawk and pro-basketball body.

                    JIMMY
          Priest.

                    PRIEST
          Jimmy Malone, you fly muphukka! Sup, my nigga?

Priest and Jimmy give each a fist bump, half hug and a back slap.

                    JIMMY
          How you been?

                    PRIEST
          Been better. Some Persian-looking suckers came down
          on our territory and wrecked our hood in Watts and
          Crenshaw looking for the Big Man.

JIMMY

Shit, fucking Asim is going after everyone. So where's
Big Billy?

PRIEST

Safe.

Jimmy indicates the others.

JIMMY

Priest, my business associates. Benny, you know --
these other gents are from the Sun family.

Priest shakes their hands one by one.

PRIEST

How do I know I can trust these fools?

JOHNNY

We're the ones that hit the Bazins.

PRIEST

(to Jimmy)
Damn! Fuckin' ballers! You the ones started this war!

JIMMY

Hey, those pricks started the war -- we're just trying to
finish it. That's why we need your help.

PRIEST

Fuck should we help you?

                    JIMMY
'Cause if the Bazins take over all of Los Angeles, they
will eventually take over all Southern California. And
that means you're outta business.

Priest thinks that one over.

                    PRIEST
That wouldn't be good, yo.

                    JIMMY
We need to get up a crew and take out the Bazins and
their cartel once and for all.

                    JOHNNY
The Columbians, the Yak and the Mexicans are in with
the Persians here. That's why we turned to you.

                    JIMMY
Your gang has the largest numbers and connections of
all the street gangs in the city.

                    (smiles)
Plus, everyone knows you're best cold blooded killers
in the set.

Priest acknowledges the props, with a smile and a nod.

                    PRIEST
A'ight, I set up a meeting with da big man. Under one
condition. We get seventy.

JOHNNY

Seventy percent? That's fucking extortion.

Priest shrugs. Take it or leave it.

JIMMY

(reluctantly)

Sixty. Plus a taste on any diamonds we move.

Priest looks hard for a second. Then he laughs.

PRIEST

Love me some bling! A'ight, bitch, you're on.

Priest makes a call on his cell.

PRIEST (CONT'D)

(into phone)

You, B.B. -- Priest. I got some cats here wants to make
a truce with us and make some shit go down.

INT. SEDAN - NIGHT

The car carrying Ken and Mr. Sun heads down the orange-lit canyons of night-
time L.A.

KEN (V.O.)

Things were not looking good. Mr. Sun was the only
friend I had left in life. And it looked like I'd soon have
to face the music.

AGENT RAMIREZ

We told you we were watching you. You led us right to
Zao Sun. Thank you, Ken.

Ken looks nervous at Mr. Sun. Mr. Sun shakes his head. He knows Ken isn't in with these guys.

> AGENT BRIGGS
> Now, we know some Arabs who'd love to get their hands on you. We could make that happen for them... accidentally lose track of you... unless you tell us what we need to know.

Mr. Sun smiles, remains silent. Agent Ramirez looks at Ken. He gives her the finger.

She sighs. Looks at Agent Briggs.

> AGENT RAMIREZ
> Fucking gangsters.

> AGENT BRIGGS
> Idiots.

> KEN
> Hey, fuck you. You sent your SWAT guys in and killed everybody --

Agent Briggs and Ramirez perk up, instantly alert.

> AGENT BRIGGS
> Wait a minute... what SWAT guys?

> AGENT RAMIREZ
> We didn't send any--

CRASH! Suddenly everything goes flying!

EXT. SEDAN - NIGHT

A truck rebounds off the sedan. The sedan skids and flips, end over end.

INT. SEDAN - NIGHT

The sedan grinds to a halt, upside down.

> AGENT BRIGGS
>
> Aw, shit!

He and Agent Ramirez fight to get out.

Meanwhile, Ken untangles himself from Mr. Sun. The handcuffs make it difficult.

He looks down. Mr. Sun's in bad shape. Blood seeps freely from a big gash in his head.

> KEN
>
> Mr. Sun!

GUNSHOTS ring out. Then, a feminine scream of frustration.

> DEJA (O.S.)
>
> Get those motherfuckers.

Hands haul Ken and Mr. Sun out of the car and onto the street.

EXT. DOWNTOWN LA - NIGHT

Ken looks up to see Deja and Rico looking down at him.

> RICO
> (re Mr. Sun)
>
> He don't look so good.

Deja leans down to Mr. Sun. Mr. Sun tries to speak.

DEJA

Shh, shh...

(racist Chinese accent)

Go join your daughter with honolable ancestors...

Mr. Sun spits blood into Deja's face.

DEJA (CONT'D)

Eww, you motherfucker!

She whips out her gun and shoots him three times in the chest.
Still angry, she fires two more shots into the dead man.
Rico attempts to curtail her.

RICO

We have to get the hell out of here.

Deja goes to her limo, wiping blood off her face with her sleeve.

DEJA

(re Ken)

Put that asshole in the trunk.

She looks down at Mr. Sun.

DEJA (CONT'D)

Leave that trash right where he is.

EXT. CHINATOWN - DAY

The sun comes up as the car heads back through Chinatown. Only to find the area crawling with Feds. Jimmy and Johnny are riding with Benny. Benny turns on the radio to keep Jimmy awake.

NEWSCASTER (V.O.)

...found recently on a sidewalk in the middle of Chinatown on Hill Avenue. The body has been positively identified as Mr. Zao Sun, age 59, a reputed art dealer, though it was alleged that he had tied to organized crime. Sun was shot in the torso and left on the sidewalk.

The news jolts Jimmy awake.

JIMMY

What about Sun?

JOHNNY

He's dead.

(a beat)

I guess that makes me in charge of the Triads now.

BENNY

So what's the plan?

JOHNNY

The same. Keep going.

BENNY

And Ken?

JIMMY

I don't know. If the Bazins did that, he's probably dead.

BENNY

No way. He's got to be alive.

He looks out the window. Complex emotions on his face.

INT. PHAT CAT RECORDS - DAY
Jimmy, Benny, Zan, Tai and Johnny and the Malone and Sun remnant meet with Priest and Big Billy.

> BIG BILLY
>
> So you must be da crew that tried to clock that Persian fool?

> JIMMY
>
> Yeah, that's us.

> BIG BILLY
>
> Sorry for Don Gino and Mr. Sun. They were like fathers to me. Where's the new guy?

> JIMMY
>
> Doesn't matter.

TONY, a Malone soldier, looks at all the dark faces around him. He leans in to Jimmy, but talks loud enough to be overheard.

> TONY
>
> Jesus, Jimmy -- why do we have to work with all these fuckin' niggers?

Johnny, Zan, Tai and Benny round furiously on him.

> ZAN
>
> Hey wop-a-roni! You don't say the n-word to Big Billy!

> TAI
>
> Have some respect!

Tai pulls his gun.

> TAI (CONT'D)
> Apologize and kiss Billy's ring, or I'll kill you right now.

Tony, stunned at their response, kisses the ring of a bemused Big Billy.

> TONY
> I'm sorry.

> BIG BILLY
> Apology accepted, bitch. Now get the fuck out my face.

Tony gets while the getting's good. Big Billy laughs at the ridiculousness of it all.

> BIG BILLY (CONT'D)
> Alright. Then let's do this. Asim's holed up in Rancho Cucamonga, of all places. We got crews all over, from L.A. to San Diego. We'll descend on this bitch like a plague of motherfuckin' locusts.

EXT. BAZIN'S MANSION - DAY
An obscene display of wealth, Bazin's mansion sits atop a low hill, overlooking the flat urban landscape below.

INT. BAZIN'S MANSION - DAY
The Gomezes, Columbians, and Yakuza are all represented. Their respective bosses, Alex, Rebenga and Han sit, looking faintly annoyed. Asim lights a cigar.

> ASIM
> Gentlemen. What's our progress dealing with the Malones and the Suns?

Alex Gomez takes the floor.

ALEX

Mr. Bazin -- reports are they're in hiding now. Maybe they left town...

ASIM

No. No. They're up to something. If we allow them to get away, they'll make us a laughingstock.

ALEX

We have our scouts looking for them. So far we have nothing.

ASIM

What about Mr. Ramon and his Westside Syndicate? Has he accepted our offer?

ALEX

Still no word. He's untouchable and has his people hiding him.

ASIM

Pity. Looks like we'll have to close the book on him. Alright then. Let's bear down and make a final purge. Once they're all dead, our position will be secure. Are we understood?

The crime bosses all murmur their agreement.
Rico arrives.

RICO

We captured James Malone's partner.

ASIM

Where is he?

                          RICO
In the basement with your daughter, She was the one
who captured him.

                          ASIM
                    (to the rest)
Well, boys -- I think we may be just about to find out
their location.

INT. BASEMENT - DAY
Ken's tied securely to a chair hands behind him. He's already been roughed up pretty
badly. Deja and two goons look up as Asim enters with Rico.

                          ASIM
Mr. Liu. What a surprise.

                     (to goons)
Has he given anything up?

                          GOON
Hasn't cracked yet.

                          ASIM
Fucking Asians. Well, keep at him. We need to know
where Malone and Mr. Ramon are. Help him to understand the importance of this information.

Asim turns and hugs Deja.

                    ASIM (CONT'D)
You've done very well, daughter. You make me proud.

Deja fairly glows in the fatherly praise.

                        DEJA
    Thank you, Daddy.

Asim nods goodbye to Ken, and exits.

                        KEN
                    (sarcastically)
    Daddy's little girl, spoiling you rotten.

Without even thinking, Deja slaps him hard.

                        DEJA
    Shut up.

She pulls a knife. Two quick flicks -- cuts on his chest well up and bleed.
    She bends over, slowly, and licks blood off his chest.

                    DEJA (CONT'D)
    That old man was gross... but you taste good.

                        KEN
    So all you've done -- the robbery and all the rest -- all
    to impress Daddy?

                        DEJA
    Hell no. I did that shit for fun. Besides, my father nev-
    er gives me enough cash. I got expensive tastes.

                        KEN
    You're a psychotic little bitch.

DEJA

I am! Before long, I'll be a Godmother, just like my hero, Griselda Blanco. I've been pulling the strings here all along, Ken... didn't you know that?

KEN

Fuck you talking about?

DEJA

I was the one who called you on the phone and ordered you to kill Tommy. You were supposed to have been shot on your way out -- a rare fuckup from Rico.

KEN

Why?

DEJA

You were the perfect patsy. Green, innocent, a complete outsider. So easy to manipulate.

She brandishes the knife in his face.

DEJA (CONT'D)

Then you got uppity. Started thinking for yourself. I should kill you right now, for Bassim. But you did me a favor. Got him out of the way for me.

She reaches down and fondles his crotch.

DEJA (CONT'D)

And... You got a bigger dick than Tommy had.

Lust fills her eyes. She turns to the two goons.

DEJA (CONT'D)

Get out. Close the door behind you.

EXT. RANCHO CUCAMONGA - DAY

Jimmy, Zan, Tai, Benny, Johnny, Priest and the rest of the Malone, Sun and Westside soldiers caravan through the street of Rancho Cucamonga.

INT. BAZIN'S MANSION - DAY

Deja sits straddled on Ken. She holds the point of her knife to his throat.
She fools with his pants. She's pleased at what she finds down there.

DEJA

Ah, nice. When you didn't hit on me at the party, I thought you might be a homo. But you're all man...

She moves down onto him. That knife to his throat is a real problem -- one false move and he's dead.

DEJA (CONT'D)

And in a situation... like this...

She's starting to enjoy herself.

DEJA (CONT'D)

The fact you can still... get it up... unh... is very... impressive. Fuck... So I'll give you a freebie, starting with this.

Suddenly she forcefully kisses him on the mouth.

DEJA (CONT'D)

I'm gonna make you forget about Maggie. You're gonna love me... until the day you die... which'll probably be today!

She laughs, and fucks him.

Ken does a slow burn. He looks like he's getting into it. But he's got a plan.

Deja humps away. She's getting close. The knife point drifts away from his throat.

KEN

Kiss me.

DEJA

Aw yeah, baby. That's what I'm talking about.

She leans forward to kiss him -- and he HEADBUTTS HER.

Deja falls back off him, her head SLAMMING into the floor. She's out like a light. Her nose bleeds.

Ken goes over in the chair. Hits the floor hard. His hands reach for -- grab -- the knife.

In moments he's cut his bonds and stands up. First order of business -- tucking his Johnson back in pants.

He looks down at Deja.

KEN

You're pathetic.

Suddenly, he hears GUNSHOTS coming from upstairs.

INT. BAZIN'S MANSION - DAY

In the entry hall, goons are shredded by automatic weapons fire. Westside soldiers leap over the dead bodies and fan out into to the house.

INT. BASEMENT - OUTER ROOM - DAY

The two goons peer nervously up the stairs.

GOON

Should we go up there?

The other goon shrugs.

GOON (CONT'D)
We gotta protect Deja.

They turn and open the door. What they see is --
Deja lying there, bleeding and out cold.
Her skirt is up over her waist -- the two men are hypnotized by the view...
...long enough for Ken to slip out from behind the door and stab one -- then turn and slash the other's throat.
Ken collects their guns, and heads back through the outer room and up the stairs.

INT. MEETING ROOM - DAY
The bosses and their henchmen have their weapons out. Food and drink are spread out across the tables. Asim and Rico are not there.

ALEX
What's the plan?

REBENGA
Every man for himself. Split.

The door bursts open, and every man inside turns -- and opens fire.
The doors and hallway wall are utterly destroyed by automatic weapons fire. Smoke fills the hallway.

REBENGA (CONT'D)
You think Asim is trying to get rid of us?

HAN
I wouldn't put it past him. He hates everyone who's not his kind.

Suddenly, Westsiders appear in the doorway and spray the room with bullets.

The bosses and henchmen return fire and scramble to get out of there with their lives.

At the French doors to the patio, Han, Alex and Rebenga converge.

ALEX

It's locked!

JIMMY (O.S.)

Allow us.

Jimmy, Johnny and Benny appear on the other side of the glass, guns ready.

The bosses just stare, frozen in surprise.

Jimmy kills Alex, Johnny kills Han, and Benny kills Rebenga. The three men do a jerky, macabre marionette dance as they are riddled with bullets.

The Westsiders join in and soon the room is filled with dead bodies. Nothing moves but the smoke from the carnage.

INT. BASEMENT - DAY

Deja regains consciousness. Her head is in massive pain after hitting her skull on the floor. Pissed, she looks around her. Sees only the two dead goons.

GUNSHOTS from upstairs. She looks up wildly.

Holding her painful head, she jumps up and opens a secret door flush with the back wall. You'd have to know it was there.

Inside is a staircase, and she runs up it.

INT. ASIM'S OFFICE - DAY

Asim and Rico, along with several henchmen watch the progress of the gunmen on video monitors.

A sound behind them -- henchmen turn, guns ready --

-- it's just Deja.

ASIM

Sweetheart, what happened?

Deja ignores him, checks out the monitors.

                    DEJA
        What in the fuck!

                    ASIM
        They caught us with our pants down. I don't know
        how, but --

More GUNFIRE rings out below.

                    DEJA
                 (to herself)
        You incompetent piece of shit.

                    ASIM
        What's that?

                    DEJA
        Nothing, Daddy -- look, we gotta get out of here!

On a video monitor, Ken stumbles out of the basement, into the kitchen.

INT. BAZIN'S MANSION - KITCHEN - DAY
Ken takes a moment to get his bearings. He checks his weapons.
    Suddenly, a commotion -- Jimmy runs in.
    The two stand staring at each other.

                    JIMMY
        I don't believe it.

Benny runs in. He's shocked as well. He elbows Jimmy.

BENNY
I told you he was alive. Ken is fuckin' <u>hard</u>, man.

Jimmy shakes his head and smiles.

KEN
We can get caught up later. Is Asim dead?

JIMMY
He will be in a minute. Come on.

The three men move out of the kitchen.

INT. ASIM'S OFFICE - DAY
Deja pulls on Asim, who won't budge from the monitor.

DEJA
Don't be a fuckin' idiot, Daddy, let's go!

ASIM
Forget it.

(to Rico)
Get her out of here. Guard her with your life.

Rico nods grimly. He hustles the screaming Deja down the secret passageway. GUNFIRE rattles outside.

INT. HALLWAY - DAY
Ken, Jimmy and Benny move toward the stairs. They're joined by Johnny, Zan and Tai.

Jimmy and Ken work together, as they pick off several Columbians, Persian and Yakuza men before them.

Two Yakuza pop out behind and fire wildly.

Zan and Tai are killed. Benny and Johnny make mincemeat out of the Yaks.

Ken has the presence of mind to shoot two more Colombians who pop out in front of them.

The way is clear. The stairway beckons.

INT. ASIM'S OFFICE - DAY

He watches the men mount the stairs.

> ASIM
>
> Take them out.

His three henchmen sneak out the office door.

INT. BAZIN'S MANSION - DAY

Ken, Jimmy, Benny and Johnny reach the top of the stairs. Three hallways radiate off the foyer.

> KEN
>
> Which one?

Suddenly, the henchmen open fire from one of the hallways. Our boys hit the deck.

> JIMMY
>
> That one.

They roll quick out of the line of fire. The henchmen duck back into a bedroom.

> BENNY
>
> We don't got time for this.

He pulls the pin and rolls a grenade. The henchmen pop out for another burst -- and see the grenade.

HENCHMAN

Oh, f--

KABOOM! The air fills with pulverized wood and red mist.

Ken, Jimmy, Benny and Johnny move up into the smoke of the hallway.

JIMMY

It's over! Asim! You hear me!?

INT. ASIM'S OFFICE - DAY

He pumps a shotgun.

ASIM

I hear you! Listen -- I got a safe in here. Full of cash.

It's yours, if you let us go.

Asim levels the shotgun at the door.

ASIM (CONT'D)

(bluffing)

I'm unarmed! This will be all over, I promise you.

Asim fires his shotgun through the door, until it's empty. He sees the hole that he made -- nobody's there.

Suddenly the door is shredded by gunfire. Asim is riddled with bullets. He falls, bleeding heavily.

Jimmy steps through the remains of the door. Asim looks up through red-filmed eyes. Jimmy stands over him.

JIMMY

That's for my father. And me.

BLAM.

Ken notices -- on a monitor, Deja and Rico creep toward a Lamborghini parked at the back gate. In another monitor, Feds and police head up the roadway toward the mansion.

Ken notices the secret entrance, and runs through the door.

BENNY

Ken! We gotta get outta here! Ken!!

EXT. BAZIN'S MANSION - DAY

Deja and Rico continue to creep toward the Lambo's door.

DEJA

You got the keys?

RICO

They're in the--

BLAM! BLAM! Both Deja and Rico are shot. Deja screams. Rico brings up his gun --

Ken stands there, gun in each hand.

KEN

Drop it or die.

Rico smiles. He doesn't drop it.

Rico glances over Ken's shoulder. Hung appears. He's got his gun out and pointed.

HUNG

All of you. Get your hands up!

Ken whips one gun at Hung, and keeps the other pointed at Rico.

158

KEN

Don't move, cousin!

HUNG

Shut up. You're not my cousin anymore. Let me kill him for death of my parents. I won't let you stop me.

KEN

Hung, you don't want revenge. It's a poison that will destroy you.

HUNG

No. You were right Ken. Maybe revenge is the right thing.

KEN

It isn't, trust me. Let it go, cousin.

Rico takes advantage of the family squabble and shoots Hung. Hung squeezes the trigger in death and kills Rico.

Ken is totally surprised by what just happened.

DEJA (O.S.)

Hello lover?

Ken turns. Deja smiles up at him. She's bleeding out.

DEJA (CONT'D)

Just you and me now, baby.

Ken lowers his guns.

KEN

You could've been so much more. All that money. All
that potential.

DEJA

It ain't so hot. There's always someone coming up. On
your heels. Always someone gunning for you. Trick is
to get them before they get you.

KEN

No.

DEJA

Yes. You're in the life now, lover. It never stops. You'll
never be free, not now. Not ever...

She slumps. And dies. Ken considers her words.

He's joined by Jimmy, Johnny and Benny.

Agents Briggs and Ramirez come through the gate. They walk easily toward
the men. The men just look at them. Too tired to fight.

JIMMY

I'll take the heat on this one.

KEN

You sure?

JIMMY

Yeah. You're a rookie. You still got a chance to get out.
Go make a life for yourself.

Ken and Jimmy exchange an even gaze. Jimmy smiles. He clasps Ken's hand.
Ken clasps his hand. The shit is all forgotten.

AGENT BRIGGS
We'd best get going, Mr. Malone.

Ken blinks in surprise, turns to Jimmy. He's just as confused as Ken is.

AGENT RAMIREZ
You've killed almost everyone we've ever been investigating. Looks like you've saved us a lot of time and paperwork.

Ken shakes his head in admiration.

AGENT RAMIREZ (CONT'D)
Mr. Liu, best you and the others get a head start before our brothers in arms get here.

Ken, Johnny and Benny beat a hasty exit.

INT. LIMOUSINE - AFTERNOON
Johnny gives Ken a briefcase of money, papers, and first aid stuff. Benny is driving.

JOHNNY
Everything you need, Ken. We'll take you to Long Beach Harbor.

KEN
What's going to happen to the Sun and Malone Families and the territories?

JOHNNY
It will take time to rebuild. Big Billy will help us out.

KEN

Benny, pull over.

EXT. HIGHWAY - DAY
The car pulls over. The door opens and Ken gets out.

JOHNNY

Are you sure you want to do this? Even if the bosses
are dead, their lieutenants will come back... in bigger
numbers. And you'll be on their hit list. Seriously...
leave town. Leave the country.

KEN

Anybody who wants to get me... is gonna have to get
me before I get them first.

Johnny grins.

JOHNNY

See ya around, buddy.

The limo drives off, while Ken is left behind alone in the middle of nowhere.

INT. BUS - DAY (BACK TO PRESENT)
Ken rides the bus in his tourist disguise.

KEN (V.O.)

I'd have to lay low for a little while. Figure out which
way the wind blew.

EXT. BUS - DAY
The bus speeds past on an empty desert road. Past a sign reading "LAS VEGAS
- 10". In the distance, the towers of Vegas shimmer in a heat mirage.

EXT. LAS VEGAS ROOFTOP - NIGHT
SUPER: "One year later"
Ken stands on high-rise rooftop, armed with a sniper rifle.

> KEN (V.O.)
>
> But as for getting out of the game... I knew that wouldn't happen.

SCOPE POV
A goon walks toward a limo.

BACK TO SCENE

> KEN (V.O.) (CONT'D)
> A killer for hire. Once you're in... you never get out.

Liu looks at the camera through his rifle scope and fires.

> CUT TO BLACK.

BLAM.

> KEN (V.O.) (CONT'D)
> Like I said... I guess it's in my blood.

UNDERGROUND SOCIETY

PART 2:
CODE OF HONOR
VOLUME 2

RAYNALDO D. DELEON II
&
DOMINIC R. DANIELS

FADE IN:

EXT. LAS VEGAS_ _- NIGHT
_S_parkling lights of _the strip._ Casinos are everywhere_._ Traffic is flowing.

INT. VEGAS NIGHTCLUB - NIGHT
An unseen STRANGER_ enters and from his POV _passes by clubgoers and dancers.

He _e_ncounters an entourage at a VIP _t_able. It's the Armenian Mafia_, led by KAZARIAN.

                    STRANGER (O.S.)
        Kazarian?

                    KAZARIAN
        Who are you?

The _stranger shoots every mobster in a heroic bloodshed shootout -- except the club patrons_ -- just like_ a first-person shooter _in a _video game.
Everyone flees_ the club.
All the mobsters are dead.
_The _stranger's _face _is revealed _as KEN LIU,_ _a trained assassin_,_ early-_30_s, Asian-American _male_._

187

KEN (V.O.)
Once you'_r_e_ in, you never get out..._ _My name
is Ken Liu, and I am a freelance assassin.

Ken inspects the dead mobsters for _IDs_.
All of them_ are part of the House of Bazin Cartel. None of them _are_
Kazarian. _
Ken checks a cell phone. _Kazarian is at the Flamingo Hotel.__

EXT. LAS VEGAS_ _- NIGHT
Ken stands on _a _high-rise rooftop, armed with a sniper rifle.

SCOPE POV
A goon walks toward a limo.

BACK TO SCENE
Ken_ eyes his target _through his rifle scope and fires.
BLAM.

_EXT. _LAS VEGAS COURTYARD _- NIGHT_
The goon_ is_ shot in the forehead -- dies.
Everyone is screaming.
The goon reveals to be KAL KAZARIAN, the last head of the Bazin Cartel.

KEN (V.O.)
Over the past year. I have been doing contract jobs for
the Sun Family and the Westside Syndicate...cleaning
out The House of Bazin Criminal Empire and there
allies, one-by-one...

BACK TO SCENE
Ken Liu disassembles his rifle and escapes the scene. However his cover is blown,
when Goons attacked him. He fights them hard with his MMA combat skills.
More Goons pop up -- with guns. Until they are gunned down by...

...JOHNNY WU and BENNY WONG.

Johnny_, 40s, Older Asian male, bold and rough, head of the _Sun Clan Triad Organization_, holding an _uzi_ machine gun.

Benny_, 20s, Asian-American male, sharp and youthful, The main sniper and lieutenant.

The Sun Clan approach Ken.

KEN (V.O.)

...With the help my family.

JOHNNY

Didn't you learn anything from The Hit Squad?

Ken grins.

KEN

What took you guys so long?

BENNY

We ran into some traffic. Funeral procession.

KEN
(sarcastically)

Fucking irony...Nice.

JOHNNY

You didn't think you were gonna go after the last of the Bazins, by yourself. We're a part of this as much as you are.

BENNY

Yeah we lost some soldiers and family. It's good to see you Kenny. Been awhile.

Ken hugs Johnny and Benny.

                                KEN
It's time to see the Big man and celebrate. The Bazins
are no more, they're burning in hell and we can retire.

They all laugh.

                                      CUT TO BLACK:
FADE IN:

INT. HARD ROCK HOTEL _- _PENTHOUSE_ -_ NIGHT
A posh penthouse is fill with, a lot of Beautiful people dancing, go-go girls and
boys, champagne, drugs and candy. Naked girls too.
     BIG BILLY RAMON, 40s, heavy set mulatto man, lovable but tough, think
Suge Knight meets Rick Ross, host this private party.
     Ken, Johnny and Benny enter the penthouse to me Billy.

                            BIG BILLY
            What's up, my Sun brothers!

The Sun Family give Big Billy props and hug.

                            JOHNNY
            Big Billy!

                            BIG BILLY
                            (to Ken)
            Word in the streets, that you guys wiped out the last of
            The House of Bazin Cartel.

                              KEN
            Thanks, but the victory also goes to Johnny and Benny.

Ken pats Johnny in the back.

                    KEN
Without them, I'd be dead.

                 BIG BILLY
Thank you Johnny and Benny.

                  JOHNNY
Anytime, brother.

Big Billy talks to Ken.

                 BIG BILLY
You think you've just walk away from the underground
society after we smoked Azim and his boys. C'mon
now, they know who you are.

                  JOHNNY
Told you they come after you, Ken.

Johnny reminded Ken about the bounty -- elbows him.

                    KEN
Thanks, for everything guys. But, this time I'm leaving
for good. Too much risk, I'm giving it up.

                 BIG BILLY
Dawg, you deserve it. After a year of wiping out that
sand niggas empire. Everything is back to normal now.

Big Billy gives Ken a suitcase full of hundred dollar bills.
    Ken opens his briefcase.

                    KEN
That's more than enough. Thanks Billy.

He closes it.

KEN

How is Jimmy doing in pen? I miss him.

BIG BILLY

Ever since he turned himself in the da feds. He's being locked up for _ten_ years. No bribe or plea bargain, sad man. He's a good guy.

KEN

I thought Briggs and Ramirez gonna help him with immunity.

BIG BILLY

They did, but the Feds are cracking down every organization and corrupt cop all over the country. They've been watching me and Johnny. The times are changing, which means we have to rethink how conduct ourselves. The game is no longer what it used to be.

JOHNNY

So who's behind this?

BIG BILLY

Some dudes name Russo and O'Neil. They are the top F_._B_._I_._ directors. They ain't stupid and they will get you no matter what. A lota pressure, right now.

JOHNNY

So we all need to do is lay low, while the other gangs and Feds are taking over our lost territories. We got to go legit now. Seriously.

(to Ken)

Meanwhile, Ken I have an estate in Hong Kong where you will be protected. Safe as can be.

KEN

I thought the Suns run the West Coast.

JOHNNY

We are everywhere in the Pacific, from Hong Kong to L.A. Get out this mess now... you'll be better off. You already lost Maggie and Zao. And Jimmy can't help you.

Ken looks sad.

BIG BILLY

(to Ken)

I hate to lose you Ken, your a good man.

KEN

Thanks guys. Better to retire early, than end up being dead. A guy stays long enough in this business and it kills you in the end.

Johnny and Ken said their final good-byes, before leaving. Benny escorts Ken, to make sure he is safe.

Johnny turns to Big Billy.

INT. HARD ROCK HOTEL _-_PENTHOUSE - LATER

Johnny and Big Billy have a private conversation at the master bedroom.

JOHNNY

So what are we going to do now? The Truce is shattered, Alliances are destroyed, The Five Empires are falling, the rival gangs are picking up the crumbs. Why'd you bring us here?

BIG BILLY

I didn't. She did.

A MYSTERIOUS CRIME WOMAN sits down on her chair. Johnny sees her.

JOHNNY

Laura.

Johnny goes to Laura -- kneels, kisses her ring out of respect.
LAURA SABAN, 40s, Russian-Israeli born Female Crime Boss, extremely beautiful for her age, sexy but deadly, she is known as the EMPRESS OF CRIME. Think Griselda Blanco meets Angelina Jolie, with Lana Fuchs and Alejandro Sosa personality. She is the founder of the WESTSIDE SYNDICATE and the one of the Co-Founders of the original TRUCE.

JOHNNY

My apologies.

Laura nods.

LAURA

I applaud you and your organization for eliminating the Bazins for good. You all did a great job, I am very pleased.

JOHNNY

You're welcome. But you didn't have to kill their entire families, Laura. Why the Women and Children?

LAURA

It's nothing personal, just business. Seeds must be destroyed or they can take root. A weed is a weed, and it has to be pulled out.

Johnny is angry deep down inside, but has to accept Laura's Code of Honor. Laura watches Ken leaving.

LAURA

I'd never thought that a innocent business man would become a trained killer. How unfortunate that he became like his father and grandfather. It's a real shame.

Johnny's face is cold.

JOHNNY

I know. So what brought you here?

LAURA

In the aftermath of this Truce War, we plan to re-organize and rebuild the organizations that's been destroyed. We'll choose which empire that will fill in for the Malones, Bazins, Gomezes and Suns for this new truce. It will begin in the future, but now not right away. We have a lot of damage that needs to be fixed and a lot families and connections that need to be mended.

Johnny is confused.

JOHNNY

Why? We are loyal to you, I thought we were safe.

LAURA

In this truce, no one is safe. You knew that. Zao and Don Gino knew it and I know it too. If those bastards, the Bazins weren't so greedy none of this would have ever happened. Right now the rest of us, have to take care each other. That's how we'll survive.

BIG BILLY

Whatever the woman says, it's law.

JOHNNY

I understand. I may not be Zao, but I am up to the challenge.

LAURA

Good, but it's seem your not doing well. Leadership is a heavy burden. I am not sure you can handle it.

JOHNNY

I am doing the best I can, considering. It's not my fault that rival gangs came in to takeover, since Zao's passing. That's just the way it goes in our line of work.

LAURA

Then keep at it. I have one rule. Just one rule only and that is this..Don't ever fuck with me and my family... ever. You both be loyal and things we'll be right as rain. Understand?

JOHNNY

Clearly.

LAURA

Billy?

                    BIG BILLY
Of Course. You got my word on that, you're the boss.

                    LAURA
Good, I'll see you two later.

She shakes hands with Johnny and Big Bill and leaves.
    Johnny leaves cautiously with Laura's Code of Honor in his thoughts. Big Billy follows him.

EXT. HARD ROCK HOTEL _- _PENTHOUSE - _NIGHT_
Johnny and Big have an uncomfortable conversation outside the balcony. Watching the view of Las Vegas.

                    JOHNNY
    What the fuck, Billy! I thought you were in charge of
    the Westside Syndicate.

                    BIG BILLY
    I am, but Laura, Zao and Gino were the founders of
    this truce. So we got to respect the elders. That bitch is
    smart, so respect her.

                    JOHNNY
                   (delusional)
    Respect?...Where was Laura and you guys when the
    Bazins killed Don Gino? What about Maggie Sun?
    What about Zao? Where the fuck were you when this
    old truce was falling apart?! Because of her, Jimmy in is
    jail, and Ken is now in the life...

Johnny is frustrated.

BIG BILLY

Look brotha, the Heat was too much to bear. Even for her. Maybe it's meant to be. Times changing and people change. It's not our world anymore. We're lucky we lasted this long, no empire last forever.

JOHNNY

Your right. Arms dealing, Terror attacks, cyber hacking and human trafficking. That's the the real moneymakers now. It's disgusting. Sweet God, I miss the old days.

BIG BILLY

Me too, dawg. But we had a good run. But we got too much heat right now, the business has to take a break. We got to lay low or we won't make it ourselves.

JOHNNY

You are right. Take care.

Big Billy and Johnny shake hands.

EXT. SAN DIEGO, CA - DAY

Ken takes a cargo boat heading to Asia, in hiding. The Ship sails away from American waters to the Pacific Ocean.

KEN (V.O.)

With the Feds cracking down on gangland in America, It was time for me to lay low...for good. I didn't plan on dying in prison. I had a few relatives in Hong Kong, so if I wanted to start fresh I figured, it was better to do it now than never. I had nothing left back in the states with Maggie and the rest of my family being dead.

EXT. HONG KONG - DAY

SUPER: "Three Years Later"
Hong Kong Harbor - Ken Liu now works at a fishing company, owned by The Sun Clan, he leaves his criminal past behind as he seeks redemption. He is a fisherman catching fish.

KEN (V.O.)

So this was my new life. I went from being a Harvard businessman-turned-assassin making six-figures a year to a peasant working minimum wage. Throwing a net to eat. It was a hard way to live, but living free in my opinion was better than dying rich.

INT. HONG KONG APARTMENT - DAY
A small and uncomfortable apartment filled with junk and clothes. Ken is residing his apartment and still has saved his cash in secret banks and boxes.

KEN (V.O.)

Don't worry, I still had some cash stashed up. I wasn't stupid to splurge my money on luxury things. If I did I would have blown my cover and ended up dead. It was not that bad overall, I did get to eat good food at a decent restaurant now and then, and have a shot of Saki. Things were pretty quiet, and that was just the way I liked it. Peaceful.

EXT. HONG KONG - NIGHT
Ken travels the streets of downtown Hong Kong -- shopping for food and supplies.

KEN (V.O.)

As for my other family. I was wondering what they were doing? I hoped everything would come back to normal ever since the truce was shattered. For me this town, felt like living in a past life, I guess though in a way it sort of was. I had not been in Hong Kong, for many years since my parents immigrated to America. But it was nice to see my original roots where I came from. Tradition I guess.

People are walking down the streets.

EXT. LOS ANGELES, CA - NIGHT
The city of Los Angeles shines with bright lights and skyscrapers.

EXT. W HOTEL HOLLYWOOD - NIGHT
A Posh a hip hotel at the heart of Hollywood. A hot spot for young, hip and famous crowd.

INT. W HOTEL HOLLYWOOD (ROOFTOP POOL) - CONTINUOUS
A new gathering the crime lords of the west coast has begun.

A lot of beautiful people at the rooftop pool party. Bikini women, Elegant Men, shirtless boys.

LAURA SABAN gathers a meeting with the bosses and underbosses: Johnny Wu of The Suns, Big Billy of The Westside Syndicate, SERGEI DIMETRI of The Russian Mafia, HECTOR GARCIA of Mexican Mafia, REZA HASSAN of The Israeli Mafia Empire...Johnny Wu, Big Billy Ramon, Sergei Dimetri, Hector Garcia...

...A new truce is born.

LAURA
Ladies and Gentleman. Now that we are all assembled here.

MYSTERY MAN
Wait. You forget one more.

A MYSTERY MAN arrives out of nowhere.

All the gangsters turn their heads.

JIMMY MALONE, 30s, bearded, buzzcut hair, well dressed, arrives as a guest. He walks toward the meeting.

JIMMY (V.O.)

I spent 3 years in the can. Got out on early for parole. Good behavior. Briggs and Ramirez are watching me. Even though I lost everything, I managed to get back in the game.

LAURA

James Malone, what a nice surprise.

HECTOR

I hate to say this but your not part of this anymore.

SERGEI

Yeah, Since The Malones are no more, we've come to takeover.

HECTOR

Yeah, your just a has-been who lost everything. It's tragic.

Hector and Sergei laugh.

Johnny stands up to Jimmy.

JOHNNY

Listen up, Jimmy Malone is part of the council whether you like it or not.

BIG BILLY

If you got a problem with him, you got a problem with me and the rest of us here. Do us all a favor and sit down and shut up.

Some of the Crime Lords mock Jimmy. Others defend him.

LAURA

Gentlemen, settle down. Nobody is killing nobody. Let be Business be business and civil for God sakes'.

They all discuss about the growing threat of the Tongs, Vory and Rival Gangs now that Los Angeles is being watched by the Feds.

LAURA

As I was saying, I brought you all here out of several organizations in the West Coast including you're affiliates. You five are chosen.

Big Billy watching.

LAURA

Billy Ramon of the Westside Syndicate.

Johnny Wu sitting down.

LAURA

Johnny Wu of the Sun Triad Organization.

Reza drinks his wine.

LAURA

Reza from the Israeli Mob.

Sergei smokes his cigar.

> LAURA
>
> Sergei of the Russian Mob.

Hector watches.

> LAURA
>
> And Hector Garcia of the Mexican Mafia. You all eligible to be members in this New Truce with the West Coast. Mr. Malone is my new advisor. He will supervise your activities from this point on. Any objections?

> HECTOR
>
> I do...With Malone. He's hasn't been on the street for 3 years. He may rat us out. What assurance do we got that we can trust him?

> JIMMY
>
> You got a problem Hector? Laura is a dear friend of my father, to me she just the same as family.

> JIMMY
>
> You speak to her about this. You're gonna have a lot of problems. Don't stir the fucking pot. For all I know, maybe, your trying to finish where Gomez left off?

> HECTOR
>
> Gomez? You did us a favor. He was never straight with us. Fucking puto deserved what he got.

Westside soldiers surround Hector. Hector fearful.

HECTOR

Okay, Okay. Calm down.

The soldiers stand back.

HECTOR

Ever since the Bazins wasted the old truce. Why should we start a new one? Business is bad these days. We've lost a lot of money. We don't want to lose anymore.

SERGEI

Yeah, since no one trusts anybody. One of us could backstab each other anytime. Reza could be the next Bazin or anyone else here. Doesn't seem worth it.

REZA

Hey fuck you, Russian. We don't do shit like that. Besides, you did us a favor for wiping those Armenian pricks.

JOHNNY

Hector is right. Why should we go back to the old ways? We got rival street gangs who want piece of the action and Feds on our tails and that's for all of us. We need to work together, for the future, or none of us are going to have one.

BIG BILLY

I said it before, times have changed. We have to adapt or die.

HECTOR

So when do you sound like Steve Jobs, Billy? Look at this fuckin, guy. Mr. Executive.

JIMMY

What a ball breaker. Listen man, Billy knows the score that's why he was the first to sign the old truce. We got to keep things in order, before our rivals and Feds make it worse. We want to win in life, not loose.

JOHNNY

I'll sign the truce. I owe it to Zao.

HECTOR

Fucking Chinaman. Alright, shit I'll sign.

Johnny Wu flip the bird at Hector. Hector just smirks.

REZA

I'm in. Let's settle this and get this over with.

Each crime boss signs the truce on paper with ink, and blood. Cutting their left palms, drops blood on the oath.

JIMMY (V.O.)

Adding new blood in a truce doesn't feel right. But with terror attacks, cyber hacking and human trafficking. Sergei, Reza and Hector were the best experts to combat these types of crimes. Looking at the hotel, we were all on high alert.

Jimmy knows that something is wrong. -- He skims through the entire hotel. There are no snipers.

JIMMY (V.O.)

But, something did not feel right. Why the hell, would Laura would host a party at a Hollywood rooftop? It didn't make sense.

Jimmy looks at a HOODED MAN entering the rooftop. He rushes towards the Hooded Man. Tackles him.

JIMMY (V.O.)

Could he be?

The Hooded Man, was a RAPPER.

RAPPER

What the fuck, man?

Jimmy checks him. The Rapper is unarmed -- gets up in disgust.

JIMMY

Sorry, I thought you was someone else.

One of the HOSTESS is about to give Laura a drink.

HOSTESS

Sex on the Beach.

LAURA

Thank you.

HOSTESS

Your welcome.

She pulls out a derringer at her.
BANG!
Laura is shot -- in the side. The Hostess is shot in the head -- by Jimmy.

JIMMY

It's a trap!

                    BIG BILLY
          Get down!

Out of Nowhere -- The EVENT STAFF, both male and female, are actually
disguised assassins, whipping out their guns -- annihilating the The Bosses,
Underbosses and guards.
     Elevators are down.

                    HECTOR
          Ambush!

                    REZA
          Get the fuck out!

                    SERGEI
          Told you this was a bad Idea!

Hector, Reza and Sergei are all shot dead.
     Johnny, Big Billy, Laura and Jimmy whip out their guns -- blasting the assas-
sins to Swiss cheese.
     Some of the CLUB PATRONS escape through stairs. Jimmy, Johnny Wu,
Laura and Big Billy survived. They escape from the W Hotel separately.
Jimmy carried Laura's body to his vehicle.

INT. W HOTEL HOLLYWOOD - CONTINUOUS
Jimmy, Laura, Johnny and Billy went downstairs to find alternative exits and the
empty hallways. Only to find Westside Syndicate guards -- dead as doornails.

                    BIG BILLY
          Shit, it was guarded.

                    JOHNNY
          Who the fuck are these guys?

BIG BILLY

I don't know.

Laura is fainting.

JIMMY

We got to get her out of here. Now!

JOHNNY

If she dies. It will be open war.

Big Billy finds a way out.

BIG BILLY

This way, hurry.

Jimmy and Johnny follows him.

INT. W HOTEL HOLLYWOOD (PARKING LOT) - CONTINUOUS
Big Billy leads Jimmy, Johnny Wu and Laura the parking lot filled with to their cars.

BIG BILLY

The coast is clear. We should separate.

JIMMY

No we stick together!

JOHNNY

If we do that, we are all dead. Billy and I will drive separate cars to lure them, while you go take her to the hospital.

Jimmy reluctantly agrees.

> JIMMY

Alright.

The Mobsters drives their sport cars. Big Billy drives a Black Cadillac. Johnny drives a black BMW. Jimmy drives his Black Mustang -- undetected.

EXT. LOS ANGELES, CA - NIGHT

The Cars drive separately. Then, a fleet of black Honda Civics follow them. Little did they know, Jimmy's Car came out last and fled to the other side.

Jimmy drives Laura to Hollywood Hospital -- she's wounded. Johnny retreats to Chinatown. Big Billy to Bel Air.

> JIMMY (V.O.)

So much for a new truce. Is it all over again? The Empress is shot. Who could it be? Rivals? Feds?

INT. JIMMY'S MUSTANG - NIGHT

Jimmy drives to the hospital. Laura struggles to live.

INT. HOSPITAL - LATER

Doctors rush to Laura Saban. She is quickly sent to the Emergency room -- Trying to save her life.

Jimmy Malone calls his phone.

> JIMMY

Hey Johnny, you alright.

> JOHNNY (V.O.)

Yeah, I'm fine. I'm in Chinatown. My boys are protecting me for the moment. Be on the look out for a bunch of Black Honda Civics.

JIMMY

What's up?

JOHNNY (V.O.)

They're been tailing me. They may be tailing you too. They drove away all of the sudden. Call Big Billy, to see if he's safe.

JIMMY

Got it. I'll talk to you later.

Jimmy hangs up to call Big Billy.

EXT. BEL AIR, CA - NIGHT

Big Billy Ramon returns home to his Bel-Air home. Soldiers of the Westside Syndicate arrive to escort Big Billy.

SOLDIER

Dawg. You ai'ight?

BIG BILLY

No man, someone tried to smoke The Empress, Laura.

The Westside Syndicate -- stunned and angered.
    Billy's phone rings.

BIG BILLY

Yo!

JIMMY (V.O.)

Billy, Laura is safe. She's under my protection.

                          BIG BILLY
Glad to hear that. I'm sending Priest and my boys to
cover you.

                         JIMMY (V.O.)
One more thing. Johnny mentioned some Civics are
tailing you from Hollywood.

Bright Lights Flash.
    The HONDA CIVICS arrive.
    BANG! BANG! BANG!
    ASSASSINS did a drive-by shooting at Big Billy's House -- killing everyone
except for Big Billy.
    Billy's phone is still on.

                         JIMMY (V.O.)
                          (in vain)
        Billy!

One of the MASKED ASSASSINS, come out of the car, walking towards
Big Billy. He is wearing a Sun Triad Tattoo on his forearm, same as Ken
Liu's, he is the MYSTERY MAN from the FIRST FILM.
    Big Billy tries to crawl to his house and on his doorstep, until he slumps --
See the Mystery Man.

                          BIG BILLY
        Suns?...Ken?...

BANG!
    Big Billy shuts his eyes -- Dead.
    The ASSASSINS leave the scene.
    His WIFE and DAUGHTERS witness the whole thing. Screaming and
Crying.

Police sirens flash near Big Billy's house.

INT. HOSPITAL - NIGHT

Jimmy listened the entire conversation. Shocked that he hear the word: Suns and Ken. Drops his phone. He goes to the chair -- burying his head. The lobby is empty.

A DOCTOR comes toward Jimmy at the lobby.

> DOCTOR
>
> Mr. Malone. I have good news. Ms Saban is okay and in stable condition.

> JIMMY
>
> Can I see her?

> DOCTOR
>
> It will take a while.

Jimmy bribes the Doctor.

> JIMMY
>
> She's with me.

The Doctor allows it. Knowing she is the Empress of Crime. Jimmy follows the Doctor. His look is hard.

> JIMMY (V.O.)
>
> I heard the entire thing. Big Billy is gunned down. He said it was the Suns and Ken. Could Johnny be behind this? How the hell Ken is involved? This is bullshit, Ken's a decent man, he would never do something like that. I am going to find out, or the is gonna shit hit the fan.

EXT. HONG KONG - DAY
Benny Wong arrives in Hong Kong to check on Ken. He walks towards Ken's
fishing junk ship.

> KEN
>
> Hey Benny, it's good seeing you?

> BENNY
>
> Hey Ken, how's the fishing life?

> KEN
>
> Can't complain. Learning my family roots.

> BENNY
>
> You realize that there are still Triads and Tongs here.

> KEN
>
> I know. I came prepared.

Ken show Benny his gun on his waist.

> BENNY
>
> The Suns are always prepared.

_Benny _grins_.

> KEN
>
> Always...I like living as a hermit. No more of the crimi-
> nal life. If it all else fails, I may go to another non extra-
> dition country soon.

> BENNY
>
> Cuba, Croatia, Dubai, even the Mainland here in
> China. Hell you could take your pick these days.

Benny gets a text message.

"A massacre in Hollywood...Big Billy Ramon murdered and Laura got attacked. - Johnny"

                              KEN
          What happen to Big Billy?

                             BENNY
          Billy got wasted. He's dead.

                              KEN
          What?! Who?!

"All points to The Suns and Ken Liu. - Johnny"

                             BENNY
          Us? But we didn't waste him. They say one of the assas-
          sins was wearing a Sun Triad Tattoo.

He turns on his Smartphone. A viral video is showing the W Hollywood Hotel Massacre.

Ken watches the video -- thinks for a moment.

                              KEN
          I'm going back to the states. This is really bad.

Benny gets another text.

"Keep Ken Liu in Hong Kong, that's an order. - Johnny Wu."
He Objects.

                             BENNY
          Ken, it's too dangerous. Los Angeles has been taken
          over by the Feds and the other Gangs. They'll be gun-
          ning for you.

KEN

I'm not going back to LA. I'm going to honor our family and clear our name. No one kills our friends and lives. This is about respect. Billy was a good man, he didn't deserve to get hit.

MONTAGE
- Ken Liu comes out of retirement.
- Opens his briefcase -- filled with guns.
- Dresses in a nice suit.
- Ken Liu is once again a Sun Triad Member.
_END MONTAGE

INT. _LOS ANGELES - _FBI HEADQUARTERS - DAY
AGENT BRIGGS and AGENT RAMIREZ, 30s. Briggs is a blond, skinny man. Ramirez is a dark Hispanic woman.

They are reduced to working at a desk job. Inactive at the field. Until, they get paperwork. Ramirez reads it.

AGENT RAMIREZ

Son of a Bitch.

AGENT BRIGGS

What is it?

AGENT RAMIREZ

Looks like our pals from Los Angeles been ambushed. And Mr. Malone was there.

AGENT BRIGGS

We got to go to LA, Pronto.

                    AGENT RAMIREZ
     Right.

Briggs and Ramirez walk down the hallway.

                    AGENT RAMIREZ
     Either Malone violated his probation or he was at the
     wrong place at the wrong time.

                    AGENT BRIGGS
     Yeah, we tried to keep him off the cage. Until, Russo
     and O'Neil stepped in. Bastard, locked the door and
     throw away the key.

                    AGENT RAMIREZ
     Yeah, it took us forever to get him out. I have a feeling
     war is going to break out. No mobster sits on his ass
     when the chips are down. They stand up and kill the
     competition.

                    AGENT BRIGGS
     Let's hope not.

They leave.

INT. HOSPITAL - NIGHT
A private but posh hospital room. Jimmy is watching a recovering Laura. The
room is guard with bodyguards.
     She wakes up.

                       JIMMY
     Laura.

Jimmy goes to her and kneels to her.

LAURA

Jimmy...I need you to do me a favor.

JIMMY

Anything you need.

LAURA

Watch over my family.

JIMMY

I can't leave you alone.

LAURA

Don't worry. It's not just me they want. It's my family, in
San Francisco. That is your job now. It's all I have left.
Take care of them. I'll pay you well. Now promise me.

JIMMY

I promise.

Jimmy kisses her ring. He leaves to San Francisco. Her hospital room is under
high guard.

EXT. SAN FRANCISCO, CA - DAY
SUPER: "Days Later"
The beautiful city of San Francisco, CA. The Golden Gate Bridge is busy.

EXT. FEI FAMILY HOUSE - DAY
Ken retreats to San Francisco to be safe, He lives in his family's house, which is
to this day, under Sun Protection.

BENNY

We managed to clean up, your old house after your family was killed. But with high rent, we had to make payments.

KEN

Let me guess, Banks and Foreclosures?

BENNY

Feds raided and took everything. We had to go legit.

KEN

So who is living my house?

However, a single mom with two boys are living there. The LEES. SANDRA LEE, 38, single mom raising two sons. Her older son SAMMY, 18, and younger son ANDY, 12.

BENNY

I'll be in LA to investigate the whole thing. Just stay put and lay low and don't use your real name, Ken. Go by an alias.

KEN

Got it. I wish I could come.

BENNY

You will, I promise you will be able to pay your respects to Big Billy.

Ken sees Sandra. They hug.

KEN

Sandra.

SANDRA

Ken. How are you cousin?

BENNY

You know each other?

KEN

My Cousin...Of my mom's side.

BENNY

I thought your family was annihilated.

KEN

Not all of them.

Sandra see Benny.

SANDRA
(to Benny)
Listen, Give me time to pay the rent. I promise.

Ken whips out his cash -- Gives it to Benny.

KEN

Rent's paid.

Sandra is shocked. Benny flips the cash.

BENNY
(to Sandra)
You're lucky that he's your cousin. Otherwise.
(sticks his thumb out)

> KEN
> (sarcastic)
> Benny do you have to be such asshole?

> BENNY
> Hey it's business. No hard feelings buddy. Take care, okay.

Benny drives away.

INT. FEI FAMILY HOUSE - DAY
He reunites his surviving family, who are to this day are living in fear. The Fei Family House is well decorated and designed. Filled with IKEA furniture.

> KEN (V.O.)
> Coming back to San Fran wasn't an option. It was the only way. My Cousin ran the Fei Supermarket ever since my family died. The Suns still protected it.

> SANDRA
> So what brings you back here?

> KEN
> I came back to the make amends.

> SANDRA
> I didn't need your help but I appreciate it, we are better on our own.

Upon arrival, Ken reads newspaper -- learns that The Suns and The Tongs are at war while the streets belong to The Dragon Boyz.

> KEN
> How often do they show up...You know?

> SANDRA

Every day.

> KEN

The Suns?

> SANDRA

The Tongs, they come in every day like they own the place. The Suns protection ain't shit no more. We're lucky they don't kill us. I pay them and they leave us alone.

> KEN

Don't worry as long as I'm here, I'll protect you.

> SANDRA

How?

ANDY LEE sees his big 2nd cousin.

> ANDY

Uncle Ken.

> KEN

Andy.

Ken hugs Andy.

ANDY, sweet and innocent. Much like Ken's childhood.

> KEN

Oh my god. Your so big now. How you doing in school.

ANDY

Straight A's. I want to go to Harvard and be a business-
man, just like you.

KEN

Aww. Now you be good now Andy. Where's your big
bro?

Sammy comes out. He is trouble but hopeful. He sees Ken.

KEN

Hi Sammy.

SAMMY

Hey Ken.

KEN

Aren't you going to give me a hug?

Sammy storms off like a bad boy.

SANDRA

Sammy, you show some respect for your Uncle Ken?

Sandra chases Sammy.

EXT. FEI SUPERMARKET - CONTINUOUS
Sammy ride with a Honda Accord with an Asian gang.

SANDRA

Sammy you come back here! I'm not done with you!

The Asian gang holler at Sandra as they drive off. Ken watches. Sandra enters
the house -- disgusted. Cursing in Mandarin.

> KEN (V.O.)
> Since Zao died. The Suns were losing power, while The Tongs and other street gangs were coming in. Andy reminded me of my former younger self...An over achieving businessman. Sammy on the other hand...A gangster, like me. Twin flames and dual souls. That's my family for you. I loved them.

INT. DRAGON BOYZ HANGOUT - _NIGHT_

The DRAGON BOYZ, a street gang that runs parts of San Francisco. They were colors are <u>yellow</u> and <u>black</u> street wear jackets, as in the Asian Race and Bruce Lee's Jumpsuit. Despite of being a low-level gang, they are the most resourceful and dangerous. They are like the <u>"The Warriors"</u> for real.

Sammy enters the rundown motel. Meeting other Dragon Boyz and their women known as DRAGON GIRLZ. Hip-Hop music playing.

> SAMMY (V.O.)
> I always wanted to be a gangster. Like The Suns. They single handily wiped out the Bazin Cartel. To us they were our heroes. Us Dragon Boyz would talk about The Suns and the Ken Liu, the legend himself. Being related made it all the more fun.

Sammy walks around the motel. The gang is getting high on meth and heroin. They do illegal gambling playing cards.

> SAMMY (V.O.)
> My dad abandoned me when I was 6 and Andy was a baby. I had no father figure. Except for Ken's family, they were honorable people. Until, they all died and my life was shattered.

Sammy arrives at a motel room and meets his gang or his new family.

SAMMY (V.O.)
I joined the Dragon Boyz at 12 out of fear.

INT. SAN FRANCISCO HIGH SCHOOL - DAY (FLASHBACK)
YOUNG SAMMY LEE gets beat up by BULLIES. The DRAGON BOYZ
come in and beats up bullies badly -- even humiliates them.
The Dragon Boyz look at a beaten up Sammy.

DRAGON BOY
Hey kid, you want to live and let us help you. We'll
break their skulls for yah. You just gotta do what we
say. Deal.

Sammy nods.

DRAGON BOY
Then, join us.

They offer him their hands.

INT. DRAGON BOYZ HANGOUT - DAY (PRESENT TIME)
Sammy gives props to his soldiers.

SAMMY (V.O.)
The Dragon Boyz have over 50 members from the ages
of 12 to 32. All Asian-Americans. No discrimination,
we didn't care if you were mixed or pure. We gave a shit
less about that. The only thing that was important to us
was to make that cash and protect our neighborhood
from other gangs.

HAL PO, 18, Thai, The Muscle, bodybuilder, hot-head, pro-wrestler type.
DANNY LI, 18, Taiwanese, The Collector, martial-artist, extorts businesses
for protection.

CHONG-CHONG, 21, Korean, The Brains, banker, he counts all the money.

> SAMMY (V.O.)
>
> There was Hal the muscle, Danny the collector, Chong-Chong the brains and our fearless leader...Freddy Kim, better known as...Shrimp Boy...Everyone in San Fran was afraid of him. You never wanted to get Freddy pissed off, he would kick the living the shit of you if you did.

SHRIMP BOY FREDDY KIM, 32, Filipino-Korean American. The Ruthless Leader of the notorious DRAGON BOYZ. He has a tribal tattoo on his neck.

> SAMMY (V.O.)
>
> For us being gangsters meant everything. To be like the Sun Triads was the highest of honors. It was like getting the Academy Award for gang banging. All gangs have to start at the bottom. Extortion, gambling, protection, drug-smuggling and money making, that what we are all about. We never stopped hustling...for us it was not just a business it was a way of life. We lived by it and would die by it, if necessary. I was proud to be a member of the gang, we were like brothers and in a way, we were.

Sammy joins Freddy and the gang to play poker on the table.

> FREDDY KIM
>
> Yo, Sammy, you're late.

> SAMMY
>
> I know, my mom.

FREDDY KIM

Your mom this.

(grabs his crotch)

Everyone laughs. Sammy Lee smiles and gives Freddy the finger.

FREDDY KIM

Word has it that The Suns smoked Big Billy.

SAMMY

How?

CHONG-CHONG

A few days ago, in Hollywood. They also tried to smoke The Empress of Crime. They say they the Suns did it.

HAL PO

Now everyone is going after the Suns.

DANNY LI

Yeah dawg, once they're gone, we get to takeover what's left of them.

FREDDY KIM

Patience. One at a time. We got to come in and go legit.

HAL PO

Just remember, we're still small-timers. We're not on the map yet. We got a long way to go.

The Dragon Boyz celebrate, by drinking beers, making out with women, playing cards, smoking weed. Sammy pretends to celebrate, but he is having second thought.

SAMMY (V.O.)

Somehow in the back of my mind I kept asking myself.
Did I do the right thing or is this is my future? But I
didn't want to think about it at the moment.

Sammy drinks his beer.

EXT. SAN FRANCISCO STATE UNIVERSITY - DAY

Jimmy Malone drives to San Francisco State University. The campus is filled
with preppie college kids, geeks, beautiful people.

He is accompanied by TIMOTHY STABILLI (aka: TIMMY T), 30, guido,
arrogant, jackass and joker. He is one of those guys you see on MTV's Jersey
Shore and Turtle from Entourage.

TIMMY T

Man, why do have to be in San Fran. Nothing but
geeks, hippies and gay people.

JIMMY

Timmy...shut up. We're here for a reason.

TIMMY T

Yeah what business.

Jimmy points at the window.

ANGELINA NICOLE MALONE, 21, sweet and innocent. Think Ariana
Grande meets Bella Throne. She walks down the college halls -- books on her
hand. Leaving the college.

JIMMY (V.O.)

Timmy T. was my best friend since we were kids in
high school. He could never though, shut up. As for my
real family...The only one I had left was my kid sister,
Little Angie.

Jimmy come out of the car. He calls her "Little Angie".

JIMMY

Hello my angel.

ANGIE

Jimmy? What are you doing here?

JIMMY

I'm just checking if you are okay. I haven't seen you in
a while.

ANGIE

I'm fine thank you. Good day.

Angie is a college student and is independent living on her own. She leaves But
Jimmy grabs her arm.

JIMMY

Is that how you talk to your big brother?

ANGIE

If it's money you're going to give me. Keep it. I can
handle things on my own.

JIMMY

Little Angie, why don't you talk to me?

ANGIE

Don't call me Little Angie. I'm not a little girl anymore.

JIMMY

Okay, Angie.

> ANGIE

Ever since Dad and Tommy died, I never wanted to see you again. How could you let this happen?

> JIMMY

Angie, I didn't mean for it to happen. We wanted to provide you a better life.

> ANGIE

Yeah, running guns and drugs and killing people. That a great way to make a living. Real contribution to society.

> JIMMY

You don't understand. This is what I do. This is what our family does. No matter what happens to me, I just want you to know that I love you. I always will.

Angie speaks to Jimmy.

> ANGIE

She sent you, didn't she?

Jimmy close his eyes -- nods.

> ANGIE

I'll see you around. Tell Timmy I said hi.

Angie leaves to take the bus.

INT. JIMMY'S MUSTANG - MOMENTS LATER
Jimmy is driving. Timmy T is chatting.

TIMMY T

Your sister's hot.

JIMMY

Shut up.

TIMMY T

Hey it was a complement, sorry man.

JIMMY

We'll keep an eye on her for a while.

Jimmy thinks realizing that his family no longer operates in California as much of them are in the East Coast.

JIMMY (V.O.)

I realized that I had to stay by Angie's side. No matter what the outcome. With the Malone's out of the game in California, at least we had some influence on the east coast down in Miami and New York. But I decided to stay in Cali, because it was my home. Besides I had responsibilities, with my old man being dead no one else was around to take of my sister. I promised to myself that I would, it was what my father would have wanted.

INT. COFFEE SHOP - DAY

Ken Liu runs into to order coffee. The cafe is filled with college kids, working professionals and hipsters. All of them are playing with their laptops.

KEN (V.O.)

Even though, I had to be off the grid. I still needed my goodies. I had to eat somehow.

He accidentally bumps into Angie -- dropping her books.

                    KEN
        Oh sorry.

                    ANGIE
        It's okay.

They both pick up Angie's books.
    He sees a vision of Maggie, as Angie reminds her of his dead fiancée.

                    KEN (V.O.)
        When I first laid my eyes on her. Her beauty and in-
        nocence glared in front of me like an guardian angel
        watching over me. With Maggie dead, I never even
        bothered with dating again. I stilled loved her even to
        this day.

Angie offers a handshake.

                    ANGIE
        Hi, I'm Angie. What's your name?

                    KEN (V.O.)
        I couldn't reveal my real identity. So I had to come up
        with an alias.

To keep his identity safe Ken goes by another name.

                    KEN
        My name is...Kevin..Kevin Fong.

The two shake hands.

ANGIE

Kevin Fong.

KEN

Yes.

ANGIE

Are you new here?

KEN

No, I am just visiting, from Hong Kong.

ANGIE

Are you one of those exchange students?

KEN

Something like that, I am only here for the summer.
Then I'll be returning back to Hong Kong in the fall.

ANGIE

Actually, I have to be at work right now. I am running
late.

KEN

Okay, I will see you around. I got to go buy some coffee.

ANGIE

I'll ring you up as soon as clock in. It's on me.

Angie enters the coffee kitchen. She works as a barista. She make a coffee for
Ken.

ANGIE

Here you go, Kevin.

Kevin pulls out his money and hands it to Angie.

ANGIE

Kevin, it's okay. It's on the house.

KEN

No no no...I insist. A girl like you in college, paying tuition. I know it can be hard, here let me pay you for it. Please.

Angie accepts Ken's generous offer.

ANGIE

Oh you're so sweet, Kevin.

KEN

I was wondering, sometime. Do you want to go out to get some lunch sometime.

ANGIE

I love to. But with all my studies and work, I will let you know for sure.

KEN

I can help you with that. I tutor part-time.

ANGIE

Thanks, I need help.

KEN

I'll see you later then.

Ken and Angie smile at each other.
The two go their separate ways.

KEN (V.O.)

I can't believe I am asking a girl half of my age on a date. But when you are young looking, you have an advantage...and a disadvantage. If she found out who I was, she would end up like Maggie. But damn, was she cute.

EXT. CEMETERY - DAY

Benny and Johnny Wu see The Funeral of Big Billy Ramon from a distance among the tombstones. It is heavily guarded and all the families are attending, AFRICAN AMERICANS, LATINOS even CELEBRITIES attending.

BENNY

Should we go in to pay our respects? Big Billy is our man.

JOHNNY

Not anymore, they said one of the assassins is a Sun Triad. We're being hunted.

BENNY

You're damn right, take a look over there.

FBI agents Briggs and Ramirez arrive to pay respects to Big Billy Ramon.

JOHNNY

Fuck, Feds. Briggs and Ramirez! Just what we need. Let's go.

Johnny and Benny drive off.

Briggs and Ramirez send their condolences to MRS. RAMON, 40, black and beautiful, and her TWO DAUGHTERS, 8 and 12.

AGENT BRIGGS
Mrs. Ramon. We bring our deepest condolences.

AGENT RAMIREZ
If you would cooperate with us, we can find out who
killed your husband.

PRIEST, mid 30s, a tall muscular African-American, has a bald head and pro-basketball body. He steps in.

PRIEST
You got a problem. You answer to me.

AGENT BRIGGS
Priest, you don't want to be a part of this. Or our broth-ers in arms will raid your territories.

PRIEST
You already have motha fucka. Your boys shut down
our warehouses in Riverside and Moreno Valley, three
years ago. We'll die and kill for our empire.

Priest is the acting head of the Westside Syndicate. Until Big Billy's brother, JULIUS RAMON, enters, takes control of leadership. Unlike, Billy. Julius is strict, mean and ruthless.

JULIUS
Is there a problem.

AGENT BRIGGS
No problem at all. It's your funeral.

AGENT RAMIREZ
We'll be back.

MRS RAMON

Suns...

AGENT BRIGGS

What did you say?

MRS RAMON

Billy said Suns and Ken.

AGENT RAMIREZ

Is that all?

Mrs. Ramon nods -- breaks down in tears.
    Agents Briggs and Ramirez leave -- they got a lead.

AGENT BRIGGS

Suns?...Ken?...Son-of-a-bitch!

AGENT RAMIREZ

Ken Liu of the Sun Clan.

JULIUS, 40, mulatto buff man, think of Dwayne Johnson meets Ice Cube with
a Kanye West attitude.

PRIEST

What's up, brother.

JULIUS

Priest. How was Laura?

PRIEST

Recovering.

JULIUS

Everybody loved my brother. Why would anyone want
to smoke him? And no one is stupid enough to take out
The Empress.

PRIEST

I don't know, he had no enemies, except for the Bazins.
All she heard was it was the Suns and that double dealing shithead, Ken.

JULIUS

I told him long ago, that the truce was a mistake. Now
look where it got him.

Priest get a call.

PRIEST

Priest here...Ai'ight...I'm meet you there.

Hangs up.

PRIEST

It's Laura. She's alive. We got to meet her there.

Priest and the Westside Syndicate leave.

INT. FBI HEADQUARTERS - DAY

A PRESS CONFERENCE is occurring right now. AGENT RUSSO, 50s, FBI
director, grey hair, white, bold and strict, takes the stand and tells the media and
photographers about the Hollywood Hotel Massacre.

REPORTER #1

Mr. Russo, who are the perpetrators of the massacre?

REPORTER #2

Was it rival street gangs or rival cartels?

Pictures are taken.

AGENT RUSSO

We don't know. We do know that the assassinations in Hollywood were orchestrated by a member of the Sun Triad Organization. Therefore, we will shut down every Sun Criminal Organization in Los Angeles County.

MONTAGE:

"The Downfall of Sun Clan Organization"

- FBI Agents wasted no time to take down The Sun Triad Organization. Led by AGENT O'NEIL, 40s, FBI Lead Agent, Brown hair, white, ruthless and calculative.

- One-by-one, LA Chinatown is raid. Monterey Park is shut down. San Gabriel is seized. Orange County is targeted.

- Several Sun Members are arrested with no warrant.

- Mexican Mafia, Russian Mafia, Israeli Mafia join forces to smoke any Sun Clan Affiliates and Businesses.

INT. HOSPITAL - DAY

However, The Empress of Crime, Laura Saban recovers from her bed. She is heavily guarded by bodyguards.

PRIEST arrives with JULIUS.

PRIEST

Laura.

LAURA

Priest...Julius...

They both kissed her ring.

JULIUS
I came to send my respects, Empress.

LAURA
Your brother was a good man. I know how much he
meant to you.

JULIUS
All I want to know is where the Sun Clan are?

FBI makes an announcement on Live Television. Everyone watches.

AGENT RUSSO (O.S.)
Witnesses said that one of the assassins that killed
William Ramon, is Ken Liu.

SERIES OF SHOTS
Everyone was shocked -- Jimmy, Laura, The Dragon Boyz and Priest.
INT. FBI HEADQUARTERS - CONTINUOUS

REPORTER #1
Agent Russo, do you have a picture of him?

REPORTER #2
Is he part of the Sun Clan Organization?

AGENT RUSSO
We don't know where Ken Liu is or what he looks
like...We do know that he was involved in the so-called
Truce Wars, 3 years prior...We are seeking a bounty of
Ken Liu for $100,000.

REPORTER #1
Sir, has Ken Liu fled from Hong Kong?

REPORTER #2

If so Sir, how are you planning to catch him?

The Media cause an uproar -- asking questions.

INT. HOSPITAL - CONTINUOUS

Laura watches the news on the monitor. Her eyes filled with hate and anger. Julius and The Westside Syndicate are ready to go to war with The Suns.

JULIUS

Where is Ken Liu? I want that motherfucker right here and right now?!!!

PRIEST

Chill brother, Chill!!!

Julius hot-headed temper burst.

JULIUS

I am chill, put a word in the street that I'm putting a price on every mother fucking Sun Clan, who smoked my brother, $50,000 a soldier, dead or alive. Ken Liu's head for $500,000.

PRIEST

Julius, you don't make the calls, until it's ordered by her.

LAURA

It has been ordered...Make it a Million dollars, Dead or Alive. I preferred alive. As for the Suns, waste them.

JULIUS

Alive?! I want him dead!

Julius storms off out of anger.

    Priest gets orders from Laura.

LAURA

You were at the Inland Empire 3 years ago, right.

Priest nods his head.

LAURA

Bring me Ken to me, alive. So he can face judgment.
Hurry, before Julius gets him first.

PRIEST

But he is in Hong Kong, is he?

LAURA

If he is, my men from Russia will hunt him down. If he
is indeed in the states? Find him.

Priest leaves -- willing to follow orders from Laura.

INT. RESTAURANT - NIGHT

Meanwhile, Back in a San Francisco. A Restaurant - Recently Paroled criminal
TYLER CHAN (The Asian Han Solo and Boba Fett), is having a meal at an all
you can eat buffet.

    TYLER, 40, Korean, handsome and cold-blooded, well-dressed.

    The waiter gives Tyler his check.

    Tyler goes to the MANAGER, 60s, Asian Lady with a thick accent.

TYLER

You the manager?

MANAGER

Yes.

Tyler whips out the bill.

TYLER

You charged me extra. The bill was 35 dollars plus the drink and tab. It's $350. What kind of restaurant are you running?

MANAGER

You bought extra. Alcohol. Lots of it.

TYLER

Guys gotta drink.

Tyler and The Manager have an argument over an expensive food bill. Until, two men from the kitchen arrive -- with knives. They are the Dragon Boyz henchmen. JIN, 25, rough looking. KIT, 23, tough looking. Both talking ghetto.

JIN

Is there a problem?

MANAGER

Man won't pay bill.

TYLER

Cuz you charge extra from shitty food and drinks.

Tyler whips out his bill.

KIT

You talking shit, son?

He raises his knife. Jin points his butcher knife. They both corner Tyler.

JIN

You hear the lady say, pay your meal or we cut out tongue.

TYLER

Do you have any idea who you speaking to?

KIT

Yeah, a bitch.

Tyler grins, he beats them up -- with his martial arts skills. The two chef are knocked down.

MANAGER

Call police!

He pours hot cooking oil on the Manager.
The Manager Screams.

MANAGER

You son-of-a-bitch!!!

She sees, Tyler's Sun Family Tattoo on his foreman. Tyler reveal his Beretta -- pointing directly at her.

MANAGER

You, Suns?...So Sorry. You pay 35 dollars. I give you protection now. You keep money.

Tyler wave his hand. He pays 50 dollars to the manager.

TYLER

Here is 50. Clean yourself up. You're lucky the Suns aren't here.

He tosses a towel at her -- Leaves the restaurant.

Sandra witness everything. She helps the Manager.

EXT. RESTAURANT - CONTINUOUS

Tyler walks outside. Until he overhears a conversation of the Dragon Boyz of the million dollar bounty of Ken Liu.

                    CHONG-CHONG
          Yo, I hear that Ken Liu is in America.

                    DANNY LI
          Who's Ken Liu?

                    CHONG-CHONG
          You know the assassin that wasted the Bazins, years ago
          and smoked Big Billy Ramon, the past week. FBI is of-
          fering $100,000 for his capture. While The Empress of
          Crime is offering a million dollar bounty, dead or alive.

Tyler freezes.

                    HAL PO
          Woo! Money! Money! Money! Just to kill one guy for a
          million?

                    CHONG-CHONG
          Yeah, Everyone from street gangs to the mob is after
          him. He's like the grim reaper of organize crime. Once
          we get Ken Liu, the Dragon Boyz will be legends.

The Dragon Boyz laugh. Until, they saw their protected restaurant is attacked.

                    CHONG-CHONG
          Oh shit. Jin and Kit.

The rush inside the restaurant.

> TYLER
>
> Time to pay a visit to the Suns. Let's go to work.

Tyler is ready to collect, he fled the scene.

> ACT TWO
>
> INT. FEI FAMILY HOUSE - NIGHT

SAMMY'S BEDROOM -- Sammy's room is filled with gang affiliated symbols. NWA, 2Pac, Notorious BIG posters are displayed in his wall. The Dragon Boyz calls Sammy about the bounty.

> SAMMY
>
> Hello.

> FREDDY KIM (V.O.)
>
> It's Shrimp Boy. Listen, rumor has it that Ken Liu from the Suns is in town.

> SAMMY
>
> I'm listening.

> FREDDY KIM (V.O.)
>
> Word has it, that the someone is offering a million dollars on Ken Liu's head, dead or alive. Are you in?

> SAMMY
>
> I'll think about it.

Sammy hangs up.

Ken over hears the conversation

KEN

Who was that?

SAMMY

Nobody.

KEN

Nobody?

Ken walks towards Sammy.

SAMMY

Man, get off me!!! It's none of yo fucking business.

Sammy pushes Ken. Ken slams him to the wall and confronts Sammy.

KEN

Don't you ever talk to your elders that way.

SAMMY

Get the fuck off me.

Sammy pulls out his pistol, as he is about to kill Ken. Nervously.

KEN

Tough guy, huh. Go ahead.

Sammy never killed anyone and does not intend to -- he lowers his weapon. Ken grabs it away from Sammy. He grabs his chin -- lets him live.

KEN

If you weren't family, you've be dead in a heartbeat.
How long you've been with them, The Dragon Boyz?

                    SAMMY
     How'd you know?

Ken reveals his Sun Triad Tattoo in his forearm.

                    KEN
     I'm very resourceful.

                    SAMMY
     Your Ken Liu. My uncle is the infamous Ken Liu.

                    KEN
     I am. I had to change my name, to protect my remain-
     ing family. I'm still Ken Fei.

The two have a family chat and sat down on Sammy's bed. Sandra comes in
Sammy's room.

                    SANDRA
     What's going on?

                    SAMMY
     Nothing mom.

                    KEN
     Sammy wanted to go out late. I told him no. We had a
     argument.

                    SANDRA
     Sammy for disrespecting me and Uncle Ken, your
     grounded.

                    SAMMY
     Mom!

Sandra leaves. Ken Follows.

INT. HALLWAY - CONTINUOUS
Ken confronts Sandra in the Fei Hallway.

> KEN

Sandra what was that?

> SANDRA

My son is a disobedient brat, stay out of this.

> KEN

Why is he like this? What about his father?

> SANDRA

He left us, who the fuck knows?

> KEN

Listen, I can straighten him out.

> SANDRA

You?! You're a criminal! Like your father and grandfather!

> KEN

Ex-Criminal...Do you think I want this life? Your starting to act like Auntie Mei. If you would listen to me, I can help him. He is still a baby and I'll make sure he does not live the same life I did. Him and Andy.

Sandra reminds quiet. She enters her room. Sammy listens.

> SAMMY

Is it true? About our family.

Ken nods.

                           KEN
          Let's talk about it tomorrow.

He pats Sammy in the back.

EXT. LOS ANGELES, CA - DAY
The FBI investigates everywhere in LA but lost the leads.

INT. BEL AIR, CA - DAY
Benny investigates the murder scene at Big Billy's House. He recognizes the bullets and discovers that the assassins are Chinese and an old adversary from the past. He calls Johnny Wu.

                      JOHNNY (V.O.)
          Johnny Wu.

                          BENNY
          I just checked the perimeter. This wasn't no street
          ammo used. This is high-grade military shit.

                      JOHNNY (V.O.)
          You serious?

Benny takes a photo of the ammo. He sends it to Johnny via text.

                          BENNY
          Trust me, I was in the army. I know my weapons.

                      JOHNNY (V.O.)
          Street gangs and the mob only use domestic weapons.
          So this was foreign made. Only the Bazins have those
          types of weapons, but we wiped them out.

BENNY

We did, every single one of them. This work isn't gang related. These are professional assassins.

JOHNNY (V.O.)

Looks like they have taken this thing to a whole new level. Return to San Fran, the heat is to high in LA. We'll inform the others about this.

BENNY

Got it.

Benny looks at the Westside Syndicate on high guard. FBI and police are scouting the area. Benny quietly leaves.

INT. HOSPITAL - LATER
Laura's Smartphone rings -- lying down in bed.

LAURA

Hello?

JOHNNY (V.O.)

Empress, We know who killed Big Billy?

LAURA

I know...It's your boy, Ken Liu.

JOHNNY (V.O.)

That's a lie! We check Big Billy's house. It was no gang--

LAURA

--Silence! I warned you not to fuck me and my family! Start praying you traitor, because you don't have much longer to live!

                    JOHNNY (V.O.)
    Wait!--

Laura hangs up her phone -- disavowing The Suns in her network.

INT. LOS ANGELES, CA - CONTINUOUS
CHINESE RESTAURANT
Johnny and Benny are at a Chinese Restaurant. One of the Sun Clan's Territories.

                    BENNY
    What happen?

                    JOHNNY
    Laura cut me off. Something's not right.

                    BENNY
    Let's go meet her and tell her the truth.

                    JOHNNY
    That's a bad Idea.

                    BENNY
    Why?

BOOM!
    Windows break and debris fly out of the sky. The Restaurant is trashed.
Civilian escape and Sun Clan Members escape -- only to be mowed down by
The Westside Syndicate GHOST SOLDIERS, the Boogeymen of Mobsters,
Gangsters and Assassins, they wear all black hoddies, skull-faced mask and dark
sunglasses.
    It was retaliation.
    Johnny and Benny witnessed it all. They escape to the back unnoticed driv-
ing Benny's Car -- A MITSUBISHI ECLIPSE.

INT. BENNY'S CAR - LATER
Benny and Johnny fled for their lives. Benny is driving. Johnny is texting.

                    BENNY
    What was that?!

                    JOHNNY
    Laura...She thinks we killed Big Billy. How could that
    be? I was in Chinatown when it happened.

                    BENNY
    How are we going to prove our innocence?

                    JOHNNY
    We can't, we're on our own.

Johnny gets a text:
    "Sun Clan are being hunted. Leave LA and head ot San Fran, ASAP. Also
Ken Liu is marked by FBI and Rival Gangs. - Linda Sun"

                    JOHNNY
    Shit! They think Ken is the assassin. But he's in Hong
    Kong.

Benny is nervous.

                    BENNY
    Um...It's complicated.

Johnny looks at Benny.

                    JOHNNY
    What...How long is he was in the states?

                    BENNY
Two Days. I tried to stop him.

Johnny bangs the car.

                    JOHNNY
Fuck!!! If the Feds or Westside Syndicate find him. It
will destroy everything The Suns worked for. Send him
somewhere safe, where no one can find him!!!

                    BENNY
I don't think he'll listen. He's back in his old house.

                    JOHNNY
Then we have no choice.

Johnny loads his gun.

                    JOHNNY
Let's get back to San Francisco, ASAP.

The Sun Triads are left to fend for themselves.

INT. SUN FAMILY HEADQUARTERS (SAN FRANCISCO) - DAY
SUPER: "The Next Week"
    The Sun Family Headquarters is decorated with Chinese art and decorations.
    LINDA SUN, 40s, Smart and strict, Beautiful for her age, the youngest sis-
ter of ZAO SUN, now works a the head of the Sun Clan in San Francisco. She
organized a a meeting with the underbosses and bosses.

                    LINDA
Gentleman, we have a problem. We just learned
that Los Angeles has been compromised. All of our

territories have been taken over by the Feds and the Westside Syndicate.

Priest arrives. The Sun Clan armed themselves -- Pointing their guns at him.

> PRIEST
> (raises his hands)
> Whoa! We're unarmed.

Jimmy Malone arrives and joined them as well.
The Suns frisk them for weapons.

> JIMMY
> Priest is with me.

He tries to calm the situation.

> LINDA
> You realize he's Westside Syndicate.

> PRIEST
> I'm loyal to Big Billy, not the syndicate. God rest his soul.

> JIMMY
> Easy Linda. If you want to go to him. You go through me.

Linda wave her hand down. Guns are lower. Jimmy and Priest joins the meeting.

> LINDA
> I received word that Ken is in the states. I want a city-wide manhunt and bring him to me alive, before the FBI and the Empress do.

BENNY

But he didn't do it? He's innocent!

LINDA

We know that, Benny. That is why he'll be in our pro-
tective custody.

JIMMY

I will do that...alone.

PRIEST

I'll scope around the city, to make sure none of my
peeps invade. You got my word.

LINDA

I'm afraid we can't let you do that Priest.

The Sun Soldiers detains Priest.

LINDA

Since your a Westside Syndicate, we can't trust you.

JIMMY

Linda, you can't do that. Don't kill him.

PRIEST

It's okay, dawg. Just find Ken.

LINDA

We'll make sure that Priest is treated well.

Everyone leaves to go hunt down Ken and protect their own storehouses and
compounds.

INT. JOHNNY WU'S HOUSE - DAY
Tyler Chan pays visit to Johnny Wu and Nikki Sun. They are old friends. Johnny Wu's house is a posh style house filled with hip IKEA furniture. It has Asian decorations.

JOHNNY

Tyler?

TYLER

Johnny Wu, my brother how are you?

JOHNNY

I'm good, Nikki and I are expecting a second child.

TYLER

Is it a Girl or Boy?

JOHNNY

Girl this time. I got one 4-year-old boy. So what brings you into town.

He came back from parole and plans to do another job.
    Johnny serves two alcoholic drinks: Jack and Coke.

TYLER

I came back to do one more job. Do you know where this Ken Liu is? Everybody in town is looking for his ass. The price on his head is worth a lot of money, and I want in.

JOHNNY

I don't know.

                    TYLER

You don't?

Johnny shook his head -- Drinks.

                    TYLER

If you do see him. Call me.

Tyler drinks.
    Johnny warns him a message.

                    JOHNNY

Ken is not to be killed but captured to face judgment.
As Dragon Head of the Sun Clan, I order you not to
kill him. He is a Sun.

                    TYLER

I will not make that promise. Even if it's among friends
and enemies. If Zao was here, maybe I would listen.

Tyler pats Johnny's shoulder once -- Leaves to the front door.

                    JOHNNY

If you do kill him...I will find you and I will kill you.
You follow the code! The Suns don't betray each other.

                    TYLER

I'm not a Sun...Not anymore. The only I am loyal to is
myself. Later.

Tyler leaves.
    Johnny drinks his last sip.

RYAN, JOHNNY'S SON, 4 years old, small and bright, goes to his father.

> RYAN
> Daddy, who was that man?

Johnny goes to Ryan, carries him on his shoulder.

> JOHNNY
> That was an old friend, Ryan.

Johnny kisses Ryan in the cheek.

> JOHNNY
> Time for you to go to bed.

Johnny takes Ryan to his bedroom.

EXT. SAN FRANCISCO, CA - DAY
SAMMY'S NEIGHBORHOOD
"A few days later"

Sammy Lee comes home after school. He goes back to his neighborhood to hang out with his neighborhood friends.

> SAMMY (V.O.)
> After learning that my uncle is a mobster for the Sun Clan. I decided to leave the gang life...But...

Then, The Dragon Boyz come in -- Meeting Sammy.

> FREDDY KIM
> Sammy, are you ready to find Ken Liu?

> SAMMY
> Freddy, I need to tell you something.

FREDDY KIM

What is it, dawg?

SAMMY

I'm leaving the Dragon Boyz.

FREDDY KIM

What you say?

SAMMY

I said, I'm leaving. I'm going to school and focus on college.

He plans to leave the gang life behind him.

FREDDY KIM

So your leaving us?

SAMMY

That's right.

FREDDY KIM

Sammy. If it wasn't for me. You wouldn't have been smoked by the bullies and we would have left you for dead. You owe us.

SAMMY

Well, time has changed. I can't live like this no more. I'm outta here.

Danny grabs Sammy.

DANNY LI

You don't leave the Dragon Boyz, until we say so.

FREDDY KIM

Danny...Let him go. If he wants to leave. He can leave.
A fucking pussy like him does not deserve to be one of
us. I hate cowards. Let the little shit go.

Danny releases him.

DANNY LI

You'll regret it.

Sammy leaves.

SAMMY (V.O.)

I do regret it...Regret joining the wrong crowd. Time
for me to straighten out my life. Good bye.

EXT. SAN FRANCISCO, CA - DAY

Sammy walks alone in the streets, with people in the streets. Until...A TEEN
GIRL, 15, Asian, bruised and beaten, was raped multiple times. Walks towards
Sammy.

TEEN GIRL

Help me...

SAMMY

Megan? What the hell?

MEGAN

Help me...They hurt...me.

MEGAN is one of Sammy's classmates from school, his crush. She is exhausted
and scared.

SAMMY

Hold on a second. I'll get the police to help you. Who did this?

MEGAN

Go to...Pier 33...

SAMMY

What?!

Suddenly - The Black Honda Civics, from Los Angeles, did a drive-by shooting -- killing her. Speaking in Spanish.

Sammy ducked. Everyone is screaming in terror and fear -- Hiding.

SAMMY

No!!! Megan!!!

Sammy goes to Megan's body -- cries and cradle in his arms.

The Honda Civics drive away.

SAMMY

Somebody help!!!

The Dragon Boyz arrive.

FREDDY KIM

Sammy, what the fuck?!

SAMMY

They killed her...They spoke in Spanish.

Danny Li kicks the trash can.

DANNY LI
I told you, you'll regret it!

SAMMY
I know where are they heading. Pier 33.

FREDDY KIM
Fucking Mexicans!!! Time to soldier up.

Sammy and The Dragon Boyz soldier up and go after the Mexican Mob. Sammy has rage and revenge in his eyes and mind. The same vengeance that Ken Liu had when he lost his family. The Curse may spread in Sammy's veins.

INT. FEI FAMILY HOUSE - LATER
Sammy searches for a weapon in the house, until he finds Ken Liu's loaded gun. He borrows it. Andy watches.

SAMMY (V.O.)
I didn't want to go back to the Dragon Boyz, but if I didn't do this, then who will. The cops would not listen to kid like me. I already had a criminal record in Juvie. This would be the last run I would do with the Boyz then it would be over.

ANDY
What are you doing?

SAMMY
Sammy is going with his friends to take a vacation.

ANDY
Sammy, brother don't this. What about mom and Uncle Ken.

Sammy talks to Andy -- kneels.

> SAMMY
>
> Andy, whatever happens. I want you to take care of
> mom for me please. Okay.

Andy nods.

> SAMMY
>
> Love you, little brother.

Sammy and Andy hugs each. He leaves. Sandra watches, she makes a phone call.

EXT. PIER 33 - NIGHT

The Dragon Boyz drive to a dilapidated pier. Old wooden pier still holds near the water. Concrete Warehouses connect each other. No one dares to enter Pier 33 -- it's forbidden.

Freddy Kim, Sammy Lee, Danny Li, Chong-Chong, Hal Po, Kit and Jin all soldier up. Armed with pistols and knives.

> FREDDY KIM
>
> So this is where your dead girlfriend was held.

> SAMMY
>
> I'm sure, she said Pier 33.

> CHONG-CHONG
>
> I don't like this Shrimp Boy, Maybe we should get the
> Suns.

> FREDDY KIM
>
> Fuck em. The Mexican Mob wanted a war, we'll give
> them a war.

CHONG-CHONG

It's not that, I hear Pier 33 has some crazy shit going on there.

DANNY LI

Fuck that! I'm ready eat some spick tacos, tonight.

The Dragon Boyz scatter around the Pier 33.

INT. PIER 33 - CONTINUOUS

The Dragon Boyz entered the warehouse. It's dark and dim-lit, filled with wooden crates and metal shelves. They see a few Mexican Mob members. They attack and wastes a few.

FREDDY KIM

You guys shot up our hood. You going to die!

MEXICAN SOLDIER

But we didn't--

BANG!

Freddy smokes him.

Some begged for their lives -- protesting their innocence.

DANNY LI

For the hood, you fuckin cholos!

MEXICAN SOLDIER

(in Spanish)

We didn't do it.

BANG! BANG! BANG!

Freddy waved his ear.

FREDDY KIM
(sarcastically)
What's that you say?

The Dragon Boyz grabs the lead shooter, CHICO, 21, Mexican, tough and vile.
He was the one who shot Megan.

FREDDY KIM
It's this the man, Sammy?

Sammy looks at Chico.

CHICO
(in Spanish)
Go fuck your mothers, chinks?!

SAMMY
It's him.

Danny Li kicks him repeatedly. Brings CHICO in his knees -- bloody.

FREDDY KIM
Danny, Stop.

Freddy points to Sammy.

FREDDY KIM
Let Sammy take care of it.

(to Sammy)
Now's your chance Sammy, to be a true Dragon Boy.
Blast this mother fucker I give you your tat.

Sammy raises Ken's gun at Chico -- Clicking the gun.

CHICO

Go ahead, chink. Do it. For your girlfriend. She was a fine piece of ass when I stuck my dick into her bloody pussy.

Chico licks his own blood.

FREDDY KIM

Do it, Sammy!!!

A second wave of MEXICAN MOB arrive in the pier. The leader is PEREZ, 30s, well dressed, bold.

The two gangs have a Mexican standoff.

PEREZ

What the fuck is going on?

FREDDY KIM

Your boys shot up our neighborhood and killed an innocent girl.

PEREZ

We didn't do that, he ain't one of us.

FREDDY KIM

If he ain't with you...Who is he with?

CHICO laughs -- looks up.

Then a COLUMBIAN MAN arrives with his ASSASSIN TEAM, on top of the crates. The ASSASSIN TEAM are a mix of races: white, black, latino, Asian and Arab.

Both, DRAGON BOYZ and MEXICAN MOB looks up.

It's RICO BLANCO, 30s, tattooed and buff. He survived the LA attack in the 1st film, Showing his scars. They are the real shooters.

                    RICO
      You boys lost?!

Turns out to be a setup on Mexican Mob and Dragon Boyz. Rico and his Assassin
Team whip out their machine guns. Mows them down.
      BANG! BANG! BANG!
      Rico quickly kills a few Dragon Boyz and Mexican Mob members. Jin and
Kit are among the victims.

                  FREDDY KIM
        Run!!!

Causing both gangs to retreat and scatter around the city.

                    RICO
      Where are you guys think your going?

Rico, Chico and The Assassin Team follows the Dragon Boyz and Mexican Mob.

INT. COFFEE SHOP - NIGHT
Ken Liu meets Angie and has another friendly conversation. He still uses the
alias: Kevin Song to cover his identity.

                    KEN
      Hi Angie.

                   ANGIE
      Hey Kevin, how are you?

                    KEN
      I'm fine, thank you. How was work?

ANGIE

Exhausting. But it pays the bills. Listen thanks for helping me with my homework. I could never have done it without you.

KEN

Anytime.

ANGIE

Since, your very smart. Where did you go to school.

KEN

I went to Harvard University for a bachelor's degree in Business. Now I am studying to get my Masters in Hong Kong.

ANGIE

Listen, why don't we meet your relatives.

KEN

Sure, but they are complicated people.

ANGIE

Trust me; I've been around with complicated people all my life. Especially my family.

KEN

Your family?

ANGIE

Yes, before they died. Well my father and brother are.

KEN

What about your mother?

Before Angie could speak. She gets a text on her phone.

                    ANGIE
        I'm sorry I gotta go.

                    KEN
        Where you going?

                    ANGIE
        You don't understand. It's complicated.

                    KEN
        Okay, I'll see you around.

Ken and Angie hugged goodbye.
    Angie leaves the coffee shop.
    Ken is about to leave -- He gets a phone call.

                    KEN
        Hello?

                    JOHNNY (V.O.)
        Ken, we need to talk.

                    KEN
        Johnny?

Ken turns around. Johnny Wu arrives with Suns soldiers, in front of Ken. Ken is surprised -- drops his phone.

EXT. SAN FRANCISCO, CA (ALLEY WAY) - NIGHT
Sammy Lee, separated from the group, but didn't kill nor shoot any one. Scared, Running for his life. He heads home by himself. He runs and hides from Alley to Alley. CHICO catches up with him -- tackling Sammy.

CHICO

Where you going, chicken?

Sammy loses Ken's gun.
The two fought with Sammy getting the upper hand.

SAMMY

You fucking killed, Megan! Die Motherfucker!

But Rico arrives, catches up with him -- pulls him from Chico.

RICO

Not bad, for a little gook.

Rico beats up Sammy. He is about to rape him...
...Then, TYLER CHAN arrives like a Rock and Roll Star -- Badass Entrance.
He pulls out his pistols shoots at Rico in the side. The two are personal enemies.
Rico runs away.

TYLER

Still raping little boys, you faggot Columbian.

Both Tyler and Rico stare in hatred from a distance.

RICO

Your gonna get it, Chan!

Sammy finds Ken's Gun. Points it at Tyler, is about to shoot him.
Tyler takes it away.

TYLER

Easy...I ain't going to hurt you.

The police are surrounding the area -- Sirens flashing.

TYLER

I watched you and your boys at Pier 33. Right? You
wanted revenge?

SAMMY

Yes, he kill an innocent girl.

He kills the lead shooter, CHICO with Ken's gun.

TYLER

I did it for you. Here's a quick Lesson...Take revenge on
your enemies quickly and swiftly. If they kill the ones
you love, you kill them swiftly.

Tyler looks at Ken's Gun.

TYLER

Where did you get this gun?

SAMMY

I stole it.

TYLER

From who?

SAMMY

It doesn't matter.

Tyler's cold face scares Sammy. He gives it back to him.

TYLER

Your such a bad liar, kiddo. Be careful of The Suns.

Sammy and Tyler leaves separately. Sammy takes his words.

The Dragon Boyz arrive and escort Sammy.
They see Chico's Corpse.

FREDDY KIM
Good job, dawg. Now, your back with us?

Sammy nods.

FREDDY KIM
Good, we'll take you home. Don't ever leave us again.
You hear. From now on your name is Babyface Lee.

Sammy nods.

FREDDY KIM
Come on, we'll take you home before the heat catches
up to us.

Sammy re-joins the Dragon Boyz. They flee the scene, before the Cops arrive.

SAMMY (V.O.)
Maybe leaving the Dragon Boyz was a mistake, after all.

Agents Briggs and Ramirez enter the scene too late.

INT. FEI FAMILY HOUSE - NIGHT
The lights are dim. The Dragon Boyz takes Sammy home. Having a little chat.
    Until they see Ken Liu in assassin gear -- armed.

CHONG-CHONG
Holy shit. It's is Ken Liu.

HAL PO
The Legend.

FREDDY KIM

Sammy, why is Ken Liu in your house?

DANNY LI

Who cares, let's send him to the Empress and get our
million.

Then, out-of-nowhere, Johnny Wu, Benny Wong and The Suns attacked The
Dragon Boyz -- with a beating. Johnny smacks Freddy around.

JOHNNY
(kicking Freddy)

So you wanna be a gangster, huh! A tough guy! I show
you how to be a gangster!!!

Freddy's is in pain.

DANNY LI

What the fuck?

Benny and The Suns hold down The Dragon Boyz.

SAMMY

What are you doing, they saved my life.

Ken Liu scolds Sammy -- pulling out his gun from Sammy's back.

KEN

I told you, Sammy not to be a gangster. You didn't
listen!!!

SAMMY

They killed a girl! An innocent girl! What I was supposed to do?! You would do the same.

Sammy berates him -- This reminds Ken of his dead wife, MAGGIE SUN. Emotions run high.

KEN

Go to your room, Sammy!

SAMMY

Mom?

Sandra shook her head.

Sammy storms in his room.

Johnny stops -- he slams Freddy through the wall.

JOHNNY

I swear to god, Shrimp Boy Freddy Kim. If you ever pull something like that again! I'll kill you myself.

Benny address to the Dragon Boyz.

BENNY

We understand what your going through. From now on, The Suns will take care of the mess you made. Your territories is ours now.

CHONG-CHONG

What the fuck man! They started it.

JIMMY

Shut the fuck up!

Jimmy Malone arrived -- dressed to kill. The Suns point their guns at the Dragon Boyz.

JIMMY

Whatever Johnny says, it's law. He's the Suns Dragon
Head.

FREDDY KIM

The Suns...You have no power anymore. Thanks to the
Tongs and Mexicans. The Dragon Boyz will never forget this.

They all leave.

KEN (V.O.)

Watching Jimmy coming in to my old parents house
was awkward. I didn't know what's going on, but it
looked like it was about to get serious.

Jimmy and Ken have a reunion -- Face to Face.

KEN

Jimmy?

JIMMY

Ken. I heard what happened.

It seems that he is going to take Ken Liu to The Godmother or kill him.

It's revealed that he is on Ken's side. The two embrace and hug each other
as old friends and comrades.

JIMMY

It's good to see you again.

KEN

It's been a long time man. You are looking well.

JIMMY

Wish I could say the same for you. I missed you brother. Thank God you're okay.

INT. FEI FAMILY HOUSE - DAY
DINING ROOM
Jimmy and Ken have a reunion -- sitting down on the dinner table. Eating break-
fast. Jimmy explains what happened to him during his three years in jail.

KEN

I hear you served three years in jail. I thought Briggs
and Ramirez was gonna cut you a deal.

JIMMY

They did but Russo and O'Neil came in and charged
me with a tax evasion. No thanks to Tommy.

KEN

Sometimes family fucks each other over. Even after
they are dead.

JIMMY

Yes, even in finances. I came here to warn you that
everyone is looking for you. Both the Feds and the
Westside Syndicate.

KEN

What did I do? I came over to pay Big Billy respects.

JIMMY

I don't think that won't be necessary. They think you
did it?

KEN

How can that be? I was in Hong Kong, when it happened.

JIMMY

I believe you, but we got to convince them in order to clear your name and the Suns.

Jimmy looks at Sammy in a distance -- reminds him of Tommy and Ken all together.

JIMMY

You know, let me talk to Sammy. I can help him.

KEN

He's lost now. He's becoming like me.

Jimmy goes to Sammy in his room.

JIMMY

Sammy. Open up.

SAMMY

What do you want?

JIMMY

I'm Jimmy, a friend of your Uncle Ken. I heard what happened to your friend. I'm sorry.

SAMMY

Your sorry?! Sorry ain't going to bring her back!

JIMMY

Nor does killing the attacker. Trust me Ken and I experienced the exact same thing you are going through.

Sammy is crying. Jimmy comforts him.

SAMMY

She was beaten, bruised and raped in front of me. Calling for help.

JIMMY

What did she say?

SAMMY

She said. Help me. Pier 33. Then some Black Honda Civics shot up the neighborhood.

Jimmy is startled. He asks more questions.

SAMMY

She died in front of me...I wanted to kill them so bad. But I never pulled the trigger.

Jimmy stops him.

JIMMY

You said there were in a bunch of black Honda Civics?

SAMMY

Yes. We thought they were the Mexican Mob, but we were wrong. They were some Assassins that wipe us out -- with Machine Guns. Some Army shit.

Jimmy thinks for a moment.

JIMMY (V.O.)

What Sammy had told us wasn't a lie. It had to be the truth; I had a hunch that they were the same guys in the Civics that smoked Billy. But what they doing in San Francisco, we didn't know.

Jimmy goes to Ken.

JIMMY

Ken, I think we should take him to the Sun Headquarters.

Ken drops his spoon in his bowl. He gets up mad as hell.

KEN

No way! I'm not going the let him be a gangster. The hell with that. I came back here to watch out for my relatives. Do you want him to turn out like us. As killers! Just to see his mother and younger brother get slaughtered. No way! I won't let that happen!

JIMMY

It's not that, he seen too much. He may be the key to find out who framed you and the Suns with Big Billy and Laura's shooting.

Ken looks at Sammy -- concerned that he would join the criminal life.

KEN

Alright, but after this, he stays with his family and in hiding.

Ken and Jimmy take Sammy outside.

EXT. FEI FAMILY HOUSE - DAY
Ken, Jimmy and Sammy leave the house and drives off.
Rico watches them leave. He calls the MYSTERY MAN -- on the phone.

RICO
(on the phone)
Ken Liu has returned. He's with Jimmy Malone.

MYSTERY MAN (V.O.)
Good everything is according to plan.

INT. _SAN FRANCISCO - _SUN FAMILY HEADQUARTERS - DAY
Ken Liu, Jimmy and Sammy arrives in the Sun Family Headquarters. They are
confronted by Linda Sun, Priest, Johnny and Benny.

JIMMY
Linda Sun. This is Ken Liu.

Ken bows to Linda.

LINDA
Rise...We are displeased that you returned to the States.

KEN
Hong Kong was boring, I came to clear my name.

LINDA
We know that. Now that your here, we can convince
Laura that you didn't do it.

Linda sees Sammy.

LINDA
Why did you bring this young man with you?

KEN

This young man is my second cousin. He may know
who may have killed Big Billy.

Linda sees a Dragon Boy Vest on Sammy.

LINDA

Great...Why should we trust a lowly Dragon Boy. They
have no respect.

JOHNNY

Listen. Let the young man speak.

Sammy tells everything about The Honda Civics, Pier 33, Megan's Death and
Assassins.

LINDA

Where did you see them?

SAMMY

Pier 33...

Everyone is in shock.

JOHNNY

Pier 33. But that place is abandoned and forbidden.

JIMMY

What are we waiting for, lets go to Pier 33.

Laura raises her hand in front of Jimmy.

LINDA

No. Pier 33 is No Man's Land. That is just is what we needed, we are at war with the Tongs and Dragon Boyz who think they run the streets.

The Sun Organization has been restructured.

SAMMY

I saw a man. He is bald and scary looking, with lots of tattoos.

JIMMY

Rico Blanco...I thought he was dead.

KEN

How could this be?

JIMMY

Somehow he survived.

There is another conspiracy, this is a silent operation and Ken Liu and Jimmy Malone are in charge.

Benny speaks on the council.

BENNY

I agree. Johnny and I investigated the crime scene in LA; those bullets are not gang owned. It's high grade military ammunition, the kind that government trained mercenaries use.

JIMMY

I checked the autopsy on the shooters in LA. They were no gang or Mafia members, they are hired assassins, and these guys are Special Forces types, real elite team like, killers.

SAMMY

It's the same guys that shot at us and the Mexicans.

LINDA

Why would assassins and mercenaries attack Big Billy and Laura?

JIMMY

Don't know. Laura's has many enemies, she kills not just you, but your entire bloodline. For business and who ever fucks her over and her family. Something we didn't do.

JOHNNY

Now that we are not part of the Westside Syndicate's circle anymore. We are on our own.

LINDA

I got a better idea. Priest.

Priest calls Laura via telephone.

LAURA (V.O.)

Hello.

PRIEST

Empress, we may know who shot you and killed Big Billy.

LAURA (V.O.)

Did you find Ken Liu?

PRIEST

No, but we may know who.

Benny sends photos of the evidence of the crime scene to Laura.

PRIEST

Those cats were no gangs. It's professional mercenaries and assassins.

LAURA (V.O.)

I got the photos, but this isn't enough to convince me that Ken and the Suns are innocent. Do you think I'm stupid?

Jimmy pleaded Laura and WS to call off the manhunt.

JIMMY

Laura, Stop it! We may know who did it! Give us some time!

LAURA (V.O.)

I thought I told you to watch over my family.

JIMMY

I am but this important.

LAURA (V.O.)

I'm giving you twenty-hours to find Ken Liu and bring him to me. Otherwise, I'll bring my troops.

She refuses to listen -- Hangs up.
Jimmy throws the phone in the wall.

JIMMY

Shit! Spiteful Cunt!

JOHNNY

Ken and Jimmy, your know what to do next. Find the bastards who set us up and show them what fear is.

JIMMY

Right, we got to be alert on what their next move is.

KEN

Yeah, but we also need hard evidence. Talking common sense and logic won't work in this type of deal. We got to prove it.

Ken and Jimmy leave. Sammy stays behind. The Suns take Sammy as an honorary Sun member. They all decided to clear their names.

JOHNNY

Time to get rid of that Dragon Boy outfit. You're a Sun Member, for now.

Johnny removes Sammy's Dragon Boys vest.

EXT. SUN FAMILY HEADQUARTERS (SAN FRANCISCO) - CONTINUOUS

Jimmy and Ken exits the headquarters. They walk towards Jimmy's Mustang. Timmy T is waiting.

JIMMY

Timmy, take us to the Campus.

TIMMY T

Yeah boss.

KEN

Why are we going there?

JIMMY

To get my sister out of the city before they get to her
first.

INT. WAREHOUSE - DAY

The MYSTERY MAN arrives, we don't see his face. Rico enters his office. A
casual business office.

RICO

What should we do now, boss. Ken Liu is in town.
Jimmy is out of jail. The Suns are up to something.

MYSTERY MAN (O.S.)

Good. Find Angelina Malone. She'll be our leverage.

The Mystery Man smokes his cigar. We still don't see his face or what he looks
like. His Sun Clan tattoo is visible on his forearm.

INT. SAN FRANCISCO STATE UNIVERSITY - DAY

Angie walks out of school -- to the hallway doors. Filled with college students
walking down the halls.

EXT. SAN FRANCISCO STATE UNIVERSITY - CONTINUOUS

Rico watches Angie from a distance, with his binoculars. He gives the signal to
drive. The Van speeds to the Campus.

Jimmy's Mustang drives at the school parking lot. It's a traffic jam. Timmy
T goes ballistic -- honks the horn.

TIMMY T

Shit! Get outta the way you fucking hippies!

The Mustang slowly drives through the crowd.

INT. JIMMY'S MUSTANG - CONTINUOUS
Timmy is in the driver's seat. Jimmy is in the passenger's seat. Ken is in the back
seat. They are scanning the area for Angie.

> JIMMY
> We got to get Angie to safety. ASAP.

EXT. SAN FRANCISCO STATE UNIVERSITY - CONTINUOUS
Rico and the Tongs' Van speeds up at Angie. They attempts to kidnap her. Jimmy
arrives in the nick of time. Shoots at the Van. Causing a Mass Hysteria. Many
students flee the scene. Allowing Angie to escape to her car.
Ken and Jimmy exits the Mustang -- with guns.

> JIMMY
> (to Timmy T)

Protect Angie!

Jimmy and Ken shoots at the Tong's Van killing it's member. Only Rico survives
and escapes.
Angie watches Jimmy and Ken in action -- Surprised.

> ANGIE

Kevin?

CHASE SEQUENCE
- Rico is being chased by Jimmy and Ken. He runs inside the campus. He enters
from classroom to hallway to locker room.

  - Jimmy catches up to Rico he scans the Locker Room. Rico sprints towards
the exit.

  - Rico goes up the stairs as he enters...

EXT. THE ROOFTOP - DAY

...The Rooftop. Rico scans the area. Look down, is about three stories high. With nowhere to run, he goes back to the door. Until...

BAM!

...Ken knocks him down. He wastes no time to beat up Rico.

He grabs Rico and sends him on the edge of the building. Tempting to throw him off. Interrogates him for information.

                    KEN
        Rico Blanco. I thought you were dead.

                    RICO
        Fuck you...Oh Shit...

                    KEN
        Who shot Big Billy Ramon?!

                    RICO
        Your Mama!

Ken losing his grip -- slowly dropping him. Rico is scared shitless.

                    RICO
        Alright! Alright! I'll talk! Just please don't drop me!

Jimmy enters, stopping Ken Liu from killing Rico.

                    JIMMY
        Ken, stop it! We need him alive.

Angie watching this. Timmy T goes to her.

                    TIMMY T
        Angie you don't need to see this.

ANGIE

I wanna see it.

Timmy T grabs Angie to her car. Making sure she doesn't see it.

Ken and Jimmy help Rico up. They tie him up. Jimmy texts Johnny.

"We captured Rico, meet us at the San Francisco Armory. -Jimmy"

Meanwhile, TYLER CHAN snipes at Ken from a building rooftop, but fails.

KEN

What the fuck!

BANG!

KEN

Let's go!

Jimmy, Ken and Rico flee the rooftop. They exit through the backdoor of the campus.

They drive off with Jimmy's Mustang.

Tyler leaves in frustration.

One of the Westside Syndicate SCOUTS witnesses it all -- he makes a call.

SCOUT

Empress, Ken Liu is in San Francisco.

INT. LAURA'S MANSION - LATER

Laura in her bed still recovering from her wounds. Heavily guarded in her luxurious bedroom with gold and black decor.

LAURA

Good.

(to Julius)

Find Ken Liu and bring him to me. Kill the rest.

                         JULIUS
        It's about fucking time!

Julius gathers his soldiers to San Francisco.

                         JULIUS
        Everyone who works for me, time to collect his head.

The Westside Syndicate Soldiers wear black hoods, skull face masks and black
shades. Armed with UZI Machine Guns -- ready for war.

EXT. SAN FRANCISCO ARMORY - DAY
Establishing shot of the historic San Francisco Armory.

INT. SAN FRANCISCO ARMORY - DAY
Ken and Jimmy takes Rico to an empty warehouse in the armory. Which is a
Porno Set, owned and financed by The Suns. They tied him up on a chair --
tortured him for information. Johnny, Benny, Timmy T and Sammy arrive to
witness it all.

                         SAMMY
        That's him. The guy who shot at the Dragon Boyz and
        Mexican Mob.

                         JOHNNY
        You sure.

Sammy nods. Rico looks at him. Ken pulls his gun -- points at him.

                         KEN
        Alright you piece of shit! How did you survive the
        Bazin house?

                         JIMMY
          And who killed Big Billy?

                          RICO
          Go fuck yourselves.

Ken and Jimmy pummel him. Johnny joins in to pummel him. Benny takes
Sammy away. Timmy T also joins the pummeling.

                        TIMMY T
          Let me try. I want in on the action.

Timmy T punches Rico in the jaw -- hurting his fist.

                        TIMMY T
          Ow!

                         JIMMY
          Timmy, what the hell?

                          KEN
          You said you would talk, now start talking.

Rico catches his breath.

                          RICO
          He's looking for you, Ken Liu.

Ken is confused.

                          KEN
          Who?

RICO

The man who saved my life, after my supposed death.
He was behind everything.

KEN

Who's he?

RICO

He doesn't need gangs to do his dirty work. Assassins
and Terrorist he hires. His name is Victor Mogui.

JIMMY

Who is Victor Mogui?

RICO

You pussies don't know shit, he was behind everything
long before that Truce shit.

JIMMY

Why would this Victor want Laura and Big Billy dead?

RICO

You tell him. All I know is I follow orders from him.

JOHNNY

Let's taking him to our headquarters.

JOHNNY

No, I got a better idea.

Jimmy calls FBI agents Briggs and Ramirez.

AGENT BRIGGS (V.O.)

Briggs.

JIMMY

It's Jimmy. I have something for you.

AGENT BRIGGS (V.O.)

Jesus Christ, Malone. I got a war zone in San Francisco and an assassination hit in LA--

JIMMY

Shut up and listen. Rico Blanco is one of the assassins of Big Billy's murder.

AGENT BRIGGS (V.O.)

You sure?

JIMMY

Meet me at the San Fran Armory, ASAP.

AGENT BRIGGS (V.O.)

We're on our way.

Jimmy hangs up his phone.

JIMMY

You guys split, I'll stay here with this scumbag.

KEN

Right, we gotta lay low, til the heat is off.

Everyone left, except for Jimmy and Rico.

INT. SAN FRANCISCO ARMORY - MOMENTS LATER

Agent Briggs and Ramirez arrive and arrest Rico.

AGENT BRIGGS

Jesus Christ, Malone. You didn't have to torture him.

JIMMY

What was I suppose to do? Serve him tea and biscuits?

AGENT RAMIREZ

There's gonna be a lot of paperwork to be filled.

Jimmy turns himself and Rico in. Briggs cuffs Rico. Ramirez cuffs Jimmy.

EXT. SFPD STATION - DAY

"The Next Day"

San Francisco Police Station, an old concrete building. Jimmy is released from jail, with no charges against him for now. Timmy T and Angie are waiting for him.

Jimmy and Timmy T hugged.

However, Angie slaps Jimmy.

ANGIE

You fucking scared me.

JIMMY

Angie, I'm sorry. I was trying to protect you.

ANGIE

Protect me? You almost got me killed.

JIMMY

Enough Angie! I want you to leave town now, before it gets worse. Head to Vegas.

Angie curses in Italian. Timmy T calms the situation.

TIMMY T

Your brother is right, I'll take you to Vegas where it's safe.

Timmy T takes Angie to her car.

ANGIE

And what were you doing with Kevin out there?

Jimmy learns that Ken is seeing Angie.

JIMMY

That's none of your business. He's none of your concern.

ANGIE

It is...If Tommy were here, he'd understand me. Better than you and Papa.

Angie leaves in frustration. Timmy T follows. Jimmy goes to his car.

INT. FEI FAMILY HOUSE - DAY
"The Next Day"
    Jimmy enters the Fei Family House.
    Ken and Jimmy shake hands -- glad that the heat is off, for now.

KEN

Glad your okay.

JIMMY

Thanks to the Suns, the Feds thinks I didn't beat Rico.

KEN

Where is Rico?

JIMMY

Heavily guarded. Going to San Quentin tomorrow.

KEN

I hope he rots there.

Ken and Jimmy sees Sammy playing with Andy. Together, they give him some mentors' advice.

KEN

(to Sammy)

So now you know what the gangster life is about now.

JIMMY

(to Sammy)

It's a rotten business to be in. It not glamorous like you see in the movies and on Tv. It's hard and dangerous. The Hustle never ends and you have to look over your shoulder every day.

SAMMY

I understand. All my life, I had no one to teach me or help me out. I had to learn on my own.

JIMMY

Sammy...I can relate to that. When I was your age. I had no help either. I had work my out own way and find solutions to my problems. My dad taught me, if you want something outta life, you gotta work at it... on your own. Independent, that what makes ya strong.

KEN

Well, I can't relate to that.

JIMMY

Yeah, your mommy and daddy helped you.

Sammy smiles -- gaining trust in Jimmy. Sandra sees this.

JIMMY
(to Ken and Sandra)

I told you, I got this.

SANDRA

Thank you, just make sure he doesn't go back to the gangster life...Ever.

JIMMY

I will.

(to Sammy)

I know you would never kill anyone. Your too scared.

KEN (V.O.)

Jimmy really straightened Sammy out well. Better than I ever could. Glad to see the two bonded like father and son.

Jimmy and Sammy laughed.

INT. FEI FAMILY HOUSE - LATER
LIVING ROOM

Ken and Jimmy have a long talk in the living room. An old style living room, with antique furniture and a tv.

JIMMY

So how long you have been seeing my sister?

KEN

What are you talking about?

JIMMY

Angie saw us. She thinks your name is Kevin Fong.

KEN

Angie?

JIMMY

Yes, her. Listen, you stay away from her.

KEN

I didn't even know that she was your sister.

JIMMY

I know that. Her mom won't be pleased.

KEN

Who's her mom?

JIMMY

Forget about it. Just stay away from her.

KEN

Okay, Jimmy. It's better that way.

Ken and Jimmy watches TV.

NEWS REPORTER (O.S.)

Rico Blanco is under custody today. Who allergy one of the shooters of the Hollywood Massacre, weeks ago. Blanco's attorney says no comment.

INT. SFPD STATION - NIGHT
The Police Station is always busy. Officers are scrambling the place, filing paper-work and taking phone calls.

Later, Angie meets Rico, on a Glass Wall-to-Wall Visitors Center. They both talk on separate phone.

RICO

Bella.

ANGIE

Shut up. Why are your trying to kill me?

RICO

Kill you?...No we just want to take you for a ride.

ANGIE

You do realize who my family is?

RICO

Yes I know, we smoked them all.

ANGIE

You son-of-a-bitch! I'm talking about my other family.

RICO

I can tell you who killed your brother Tommy?

ANGIE

I know who did. The Bazins did it.

RICO

It wasn't us or the Bazins, chica.

ANGIE

Who?

Rico smiles -- whispers on the phone.

Angie's face is shocked -- drops the phone. She quick runs out of the building.
Rico laughs, as he reveals to Angie the truth.

INT. FEI FAMILY HOUSE - NIGHT

Ken sleeps in his bedroom. A SHADOW FIGURE appears. He attempts to
shoot Ken.

Ken wrestle with the shooter -- dropping the gun. Jimmy wakes up -- turns
on the lights. The Shadow Figure...

...It's ANGIE.

KEN

Angie?!

Angie confronts Ken and in a fit of rage she tries to kill him. Jimmy stops her.
Restrains her.

JIMMY

Angie stop it.

ANGIE

He killed Tommy! My brother and yours! How could
you team up with this murderer!

JIMMY

Angie! It's not what you think!

Jimmy stops her.

KEN

Jimmy, I'll explain to her!

ANGIE

Yeah tell me you bastard. Kevin or Ken Liu, if that's your name.

KEN

It is. I'm not Kevin Fong...I'm Ken Liu of The Sun Triads.

Timmy T arrives. Sandra wakes up.

KEN

If you had someone you love...Die in the hands of one of your supposed ally. What would you do? Tommy and Deja took everything from me and now I am in this life. They knew. I knew. Yes I killed Tommy.

Andy and Sammy watches. Sandra pulls them away.

JIMMY

Listen, I hated it as much as you do Angie. But Tommy was lost and betrayed us all, Papa don't recognize him anymore.

ANGIE

Your lying...YOUR ALL LYING!!!

Angie refuses to listen -- Storms off in Emotion. Cursing in Italian.

TIMMY T

I tried to stop her.

JIMMY

You had one job Timmy.

Jimmy shook his head at Timmy T.

TIMMY T

She wouldn't listen to me. What the fuck was I supposed to do!

Timmy T leaves to look out for her.

JIMMY (V.O.)

I didn't blame Angie for getting angry. I was angry
at Ken too, back then. But I learned how to accept
Tommy's betrayal. Unfortunately, Angie would never
understand.

EXT. FEI FAMILY HOUSE -_ BACKYARD -_ NIGHT
Jimmy is all alone looking at the stars in the sky. He prays to God.
Ken comes outside. To join Jimmy.

KEN

Looks like your sister hates me, now.

JIMMY

Us, Ken. She hates us.

KEN

You're her older brother.

Jimmy sighs.

JIMMY

I am her brother, but not a good one. Tommy was the
one who was nice to her. Her loved her very much.

                    KEN
Why him? He's was a bastard.

Jimmy tells the story of his family.

                    JIMMY
Tommy was not always born a bastard. He was made
one.

                    KEN

    How?

FLASHBACK
INT. HOSPITAL - NIGHT
"1995"
    YOUNG LAURA, Beautiful, before she became the Empress of Crime, is
giving birth to BABY ANGIE, in a private room. YOUNG GINO, Handsome
was still an Underboss, arrives. They embrace their newborn child. The two
agreed to keep it secret.

                    JIMMY (V.O.)
My father told me that he had an affair with a Drug
Lord's daughter. The two were in love. She gave birth
to Angie, my sister.

Two Crime Bosses, DON ROBERTO MANZINI and MR. SABAN arrives.
_[[is the flashback over? say so if so]]

INT. HOSPITAL - MOMENTS LATER
Don Roberto and Mr. Saban have an argument with Young Gino and Young
Laura. The two kept quiet about Angie's birth.

JIMMY (V.O.)
My grandfather and Mr. Saban were rivals in organized
crime.

To keep the alliances intact. Don Roberto allows Young Gino to take Angie into
his custody. Mr. Saban, was the EMPEROR OF CRIME in the WEST COAST,
wanted Angie dead, but Laura begged him not to.

JIMMY (V.O.)
Mr. Saban use to run the biggest criminal organization
in the west coast. Seeing Angie as an abomination, he
wanted her dead.

Mr. Saban agrees with her daughter, but she is no longer allowed to see The
Malones or Angie ever again.
FLASHBACK_: - The Past

INT. MALONE COMPOUND - DAY
Young Gino brings in Baby Angie to the Malone Family.

JIMMY (V.O.)
But, my father was able to hide her.

MARY MANZINI-MALONE, the mother of Jimmy and Tommy, was infertile
after Tommy's birth. Is glad to have a daughter now. TEENAGE JIMMY and
YOUNG TOMMY embraced their new sister.

JIMMY (V.O.)
My mom never found out the truth, but she embraced
Angie as her own. Dad told her that he found her in an
adoption agency.

EXT. MALONE COMPOUND - DAY
"Summer 2000"

    Young Gino, Mary, Jimmy, Tommy and Angie are having a family barbecue. Several families joined. Kids were playing. Adult are socializing.

> JIMMY (V.O.)
>
> We were all living peacefully. I wanted to go to business school.

    Jimmy is playing with Angie, now 5 and her friends.
    Tommy is hanging out with bad kids -- smoking weed from the back.

> JIMMY (V.O.)
>
> Tommy on the other hand...Well he joined the wrong crowd.

    Jimmy sees Tommy. Scaring off the bad kids. Tommy and Jimmy fight. Mary breaks them up -- scolds them.

> JIMMY (V.O.)
>
> We had a happy family...sometimes.

    A RIVAL MAFIA GANG arrive and shot up the Malone Compound.

> JIMMY (V.O.)
>
> Until everything changed.

    Everyone hides. Gino and his men defend their home -- wasting them. Jimmy helps his dad. Tommy protects Angie. Mary was the only causality. This traumatized Tommy.
    Gino checks the Identifications of the shooters. It was MR. SABAN men.

> JIMMY (V.O.)
>
> Mr. Saban somehow found out that Angie is still alive,
> he ordered the hit.

Young Gino is going after Mr. Saban, Jimmy joins him, much to Gino's dismay.

EXT. SABAN'S MANSION - NIGHT
YOUNG GINO and TEEN JIMMY is about to enter MR. SABAN'S Mansion, to retaliate.

> JIMMY (V.O.)
>
> My dad and I decide to take out Mr. Saban. However,
> it didn't happen.

However a group of Asian Men stop them. ZAO SUN, Head of the Sun Clan appears. Along with a YOUNG JOHNNY WU and YOUNG TYLER CHAN.

> JIMMY (V.O.)
>
> Zao, stops us. He informed us that Mr. Saban's death
> was taken care of.

INT. SABAN'S MANSION - NIGHT
Young Laura poisons her Father to death. After attempting to kill her own granddaughter. She is determined to get her daughter back.

INT. MALONE COMPOUND - DAY
After the Mary's Funeral. Zao Sun, Underboss Gino, Don Roberto, Big Billy and Laura have all decided to cease fire and began the TRUCE.

> JIMMY (V.O.)
>
> With Mr. Saban outta the way. The crime lords decided
> to put an end of the wars. They formed the Truce.

INT. MALONE COMPOUND - MOMENTS LATER
YOUNG LAURA arrives, with guards and lawyers, to reclaim her Daughter, ANGIE. Now she is The Empress of Crime.

> JIMMY (V.O.)
> One of the terms was for Laura to have full custody of Angie. She would become the Empress of Crime and we would have visitation rights to see my little sister.

LITTLE ANGIE cries. YOUNG TOMMY tries to hold Angie -- was pulled back.

TEEN JIMMY, understands, powerless to stop her, he joins the family business to protect his family. GINO reluctantly agrees for Jimmy to join the family business.

> JIMMY (V.O.)
> Losing Angie, affected us all. It changed us.

Without Angie, Tommy went psycho.

> JIMMY
> It drove my brother insane. It broke him to pieces. That's why he became so fucked up.

EXT. FEI FAMILY HOUSE - NIGHT (PRESENT TIME)
Jimmy finishes the story of Angie and the Truce.

> KEN
> So that's how the Truce was formed, Because of Angie.

Jimmy nods.

KEN

I didn't know that Tommy had a good side to him. Shit, now I regret killing him for what he did.

JIMMY

That is why I have to protect Angie. If something happens to her, Laura will smoke every gang in the West Coast to avenge her. It would be like a Mafia World War.

KEN

How powerful is she?

JIMMY

Let's say she's worth billions. Her father was an Oil and Opium Tycoon. Her father was Bazin's partner at one time. Think the Warren Buffet of Drug Lords and shady investments.

KEN

Look, I think we should go get some sleep good night.

Ken leaves.

JIMMY
(sarcastically)

Get some z's fucko.

Ken laugh.

KEN

You too. Smart ass.

Jimmy stays outside, thinking.

INT. ANGIE'S APARTMENT - DAY
"The Next Day"

Jimmy goes to Angie's Apartment. It was trashed. Bookshelves and litter is all over the place. He finds Timmy T beaten up.

JIMMY
Shit, Timmy! Who did this?

TIMMY T
Fucking Tongs. Outnumbering me like ants.

Angie Screams off screen.

EXT. ANGIE'S APARTMENT - CONTINUOUS
Jimmy goes outside and sees Tong members grabbing Angie sending her in the trunk.

JIMMY
Angie!

ANGIE
Jimmy, Help me!

The trunk shuts close. The Tongs speak in Cantonese.
He quickly goes to his car and chases them.

EXT. SAN FRANCISCO, CA - CONTINUOUS
CAR CHASE
- Jimmy's Mustang chases Tong Supercars - Honda Civics. He is able to ram a few of them down. He pulls out his rifle shoots them down.
    - The Mustang and the Civic drive through long hills of San Francisco.
    - The Mustang catches up to the Lead Civic -- The One that has Angie.
    - Suddenly, A Dodge Ram truck crashes through Jimmy's Mustang on the side. Completely totaling the car.

- The Civic and Ram successfully get away.

- Jimmy Malone barely survive. Priest arrives in time to save his brother-in-arms.

PRIEST

You alright, man.

JIMMY

No, they got my sister. They fucked with the wrong family.

PRIEST

I hate to tell you this but my Westside brothers are in town.

JIMMY

We got to warn Ken and The Suns.

PRIEST

Ai'ight.

Jimmy and Priest leave.

EXT. FEI SUPERMARKET - DAY
Ken Liu goes to his supermarket to check his Cousin Sandra.

INT. FEI SUPERMARKET - CONTINUOUS
Sandra is stocking supplies in a small Asian supermarket. A convenient store like the Kwik-E-Mart from "The Simpsons".

KEN

Sandra. This is important.

> SANDRA

What is it?

> KEN

Johnny Wu has arranged for you, Andy and Sammy to flee to Seattle where it's safe. You can't stay here anymore, it's too dangerous.

> SANDRA

I'm not going anywhere, this is my home.

> KEN

You have no choice. The heat is too high for us.

EXT. FEI SUPERMARKET - CONTINUOUS
The Tongs blow up his BMW Car. Everyone jumped to the floor.

Tyler Chan arrives as he and Ken Liu have a brief kung fu fight, leaving Tyler the victor, ready to kill Ken.

> TYLER

Time to collect.

But JULIUS and the Westside Syndicate arrives and goes after Ken.

> JULIUS

Smoke that fool!

Johnny and The Suns, arrive in the nick of time -- allowing Ken to escape.

EXT. ALLEY WAY - CONTINUOUS
Tyler Chan catches up with him, about to collect the bounty and send him to Laura for judgment but is stopped by Johnny Wu.

JOHNNY

If your going to get him, you go through me.

TYLER

I'll take you both on. I told you to stay outta my way.

JOHNNY

Tyler, stop it.

Johnny points his gun at Tyler -- not afraid to smoke his friend.

JOHNNY

We know who it behind this, It's not us. It's the Tongs who are behind Big Billy's assassination.

TYLER

I don't care. All I came for is the bounty and my money. Zao's not here to save you now.

JOHNNY

But he wouldn't approve of it. Listen, we can take down the Tongs and their allies, you'll get more money than the bounty on Ken. You were a Sun once, a code of honor that we followed. Don't you remember?

Tyler puts his gun away -- sparing Ken.

TYLER

Your on your own. You bought yourselves 24 hours.

Tyler leaves. Johnny helps Ken. Ken's phone rings.

KEN

Hello?

MYSTERY MAN (V.O.)
Ken Liu...I've been waiting for you.

KEN
Who is this?

MYSTERY MAN
Meet me at Pier 33 and will have a little chat.

Ken hangs up.

KEN
I have to go to Pier 33.

JOHNNY
We are coming with you. We'll make sure Sandra and
Andy head to Seattle.

ACT THREE

INT. PIER 33 - DAY
Angie is held hostage by the Tongs. Victor Mogui, unseen, confronts her.

VICTOR
Welcome, Miss Malone.

ANGIE
Who are you?

VICTOR
It doesn't matter.

ANGIE
You bastards, you know who my mother is and my
family. They will hunt you down til you are dead.

Victor smacks her in the face.

                    VICTOR
        I am expecting that!

A Slave Trade known as TIGER LADY, 60s, mean and tough, chaining several YOUNG GIRLS.

                    TIGER LADY
        What should we do with Angie? Should she be sold to
        the Arabs and Europeans?

                    VICTOR
        No. Send her to my room. I have plans for her.

Tiger Lady grabs Angie away and takes her to the Storage Room.

                    ANGIE
        No! You bastard!

INT. SUN FAMILY HEADQUARTERS (SAN FRANCISCO) - DAY
Ken, The Suns, Priest and Jimmy Malone have a group meeting. They discover the Tong hideout...Pier 33.

                    JIMMY
        Damn you look like hell?

                    KEN
        You don't look so good yourself.

                    JIMMY
        They got Angie.

                              KEN
Shit. We'll let's go save her.

                             JIMMY
How's your family?

                              KEN
Their heading to Seattle.

Johnny and Linda leads the team.

                            JOHNNY
We got all the evidence we need to clear our names.
Unfortunately, the Feds won't buy it.

                         AGENT BRIGGS
Sure we will.

Briggs and Ramirez arrive. The Gangsters look at them -- ready to fight.

                             LINDA
Feds, you have no jurisdiction on us.

                        AGENT RAMIREZ
We didn't came to prosecute you. We came to help. All
we need is more hard evidence and we can clear your
names.

                             JIMMY
If you do that, can you clear Ken Liu's name?

                         AGENT BRIGGS
I can't promise you that.

JIMMY

Take it or leave it.

AGENT RAMIREZ

Have it your way, Malone.

Linda calls Laura and sends them more evidence.

Ramirez places a wire, disguised as Mp3 Player on Ken.

Laura is convinced that it was the Victor and assassins. Victor's private army.

LINDA

Laura, here is the evidence that clears our names. It's Victor Mogui and the Tongs that were behind the assassination.

LAURA (V.O.)

I am convinced now. Victor is a dangerous man, he has no honor. He wiped out a small village in Ukraine, years ago. What about my family, are they protected?

Jimmy hesitates.

JIMMY

Yeah, they're alright.

LAURA

Good. I authorize the execution of Victor Mogui, his army and his family. Do it quick before the Feds catch up to you. I am calling off the bounty on Ken Liu and the Suns. For now you are all cleared. Kill Victor that is my order!

JOHNNY

Thank you, we will hunt them down.

Laura hangs up.

PRIEST
I am going to convince Julius and tell him the truth.
For all I know is he is smoking every Sun member.

Who are behind the attacks, she orders their execution, much like the Bazins.

AGENT BRIGGS
Looks like our brother-in-arms are coming in hard on
The Suns. We will lure them to Pier 33.

AGENT RAMIREZ
And we we'll make sure you are all safe. We won't be
liable though, if you are killed or arrested.

LINDA
Hurry, we have to leave before the Feds find out about
this place.

EXT. SUN FAMILY HEADQUARTERS (SAN FRANCISCO) - DAY
Briggs, Ramirez, The Suns, Priest, Jimmy and Ken all leave their last stronghold.
    In order to cover up their criminal activities. Linda detonates a bomb.
    BOOM!
    The Sun Clan Compound is completely blown up. Destroying everything.
    The Cars drive away.

EXT. SAN FRANCISCO, CA - DAY
MONTAGE - FBI Raids
"Ready or Not" by The Fugees plays.
    FBI are taking down on every gang in the west coast. Special Agent Max
Russo and Nick O'Neil, they wasted no time of arresting every gang in the na-
tion. Only the Dragon Boyz escape.

Tyler watches FBI Raids on gangs and criminals -- like a witchhunt. Clearly sees what's going on.

INT. DRAGON BOYZ HANGOUT - DAY
Every Dragon Boy and Dragon Girl scramble, ready to leave. Sammy is looking for Freddy Kim.

> FREDDY KIM
> What the fuck are you doing here? The cops and Feds are cleaning house.

> SAMMY
> I didn't came to come back to join you. I came for your guys help.

> FREDDY KIM
> Why should we?

> SAMMY
> My uncle is Ken Liu. He is going to Pier 33 to do something big and needs more men to help.

> FREDDY KIM
> Are you fucking kidding me? That's suicide, we almost got smoked there.

> SAMMY
> This time they got all the firepower and money to take them out.

> FREDDY KIM
> Sorry, man. This is our turf. We don't do shit like that.

> SAMMY

If your so tough and people fear you, how come your chickening out? Your Shrimp Boy Freddy Kim, the head of the Dragon Boyz, if it weren't for you guys, I would have been beaten up or dead.

The Dragon Boyz starting to listen.

> SAMMY

Laura called off the hunt and declared the Tongs are the shooters of her and Big Billy. If we don't help Ken and the Suns, there is no home to go back to.

Danny Li, Chong-Chong and Hal Po, sided with Benny.

> DANNY LI

He's right. The Tongs been stepping on us for years. Time to return the favor.

> CHONG-CHONG

We kept peace in this neighborhood for years. We're here to protect, not take.

> HAL PO

We were poor Asian kids, who wanted a piece of the action, not to fight the whole world.

> SAMMY

This could be your chance to go big time and be part of the Laura's network of crime.

Freddy Kim thinks.

EXT. PIER 33 - NIGHT
Ken Liu arrives at The Tong compound in a warehouse dock and pier to confront them.

                    KEN
    I'm here!

                    VICTOR
    Come inside...Alone.

The Door opens. Ken enters.
    Under the docks -- The Sun Clan emerges from the water, like navy seals. They secretly dispose of the Tong Soldiers and Terrorists.

INT. PIER 33 - CONTINUOUS
Ken and Victor finally meet.
    VICTOR MOGUI, is revealed, half-white and half-Asian, looks like Keanu Reeves. He is behind the conspiracy. The MYSTERY MAN from the first film.

                    VICTOR
    Hello, Liu.

                    KEN
    You know me.

                    VICTOR
    I know your family. Ken Fei. You think hiding would
    escape this. No, your born with this curse.

                    KEN
    How'd you know my family, Victor? And where is
    Angie?

VICTOR

I'll tell you everything.

Victor reveals everything to Ken, shows his sun tattoo on his arm. The same as Ken's arm -- He used it to frame him.
FLASHBACK

INT. SUN FAMILY HEADQUARTERS (SAN FRANCISCO) - NIGHT
Victor was once a Sun member until Zao banned him due to being too violent and dishonorable.

VICTOR (V.O.)

I was Zao's best student but he expelled me for being
too violent and cruel.

INT. TONG HEADQUARTERS - NIGHT
Victor plans to wipe out every gang in America, along with the Tongs and expand all over the USA.

They have completely taken over much of the west coast by eliminating the competition:

INT. PIER 33 - NIGHT

KEN

Skip it. Why me?

VICTOR

I orchestrated this years ago, starting with the breaking
of the Truce.

MONTAGE FLASHBACK:
Victor was the mastermind of everything happen to Ken Liu's life.
- Assassinating Ken's Family.

VICTOR

Your family dishonored me. So I killed them.

KEN

How did I dishonored you?

VICTOR

I was 5 when my family and Tong Family was taken away from me. By your father and grandfather. When I grew up, I joined the Suns to infiltrate them just to track you guys down. It took years but it's worth it.

- The LA Art Gallery robbery scene (which Victor the mastermind)

VICTOR

The Art Gallery heist was my idea and I took the money that was owed to me.

- Blowing up the Malone Storehouses (which Victor planted the bombs)

VICTOR

The Suns allies are my enemies.

- Manipulating Tommy Malone at the bar where Liu was drinking (which Victor grabbed Tommy and made him beg)

VICTOR

Tommy was a prick, I had pleasure to corrupt him.

- Convincing The Gomezs and Yakuza to side with the Bazins.

VICTOR

The Bazins and I convinced the other gangs to join us.

- Deja's lover (Victor's true lover is Deja Bazin)

VICTOR

Deja and I were engaged. Until, you took her from me.

- He killed The Mings in Monterey Park. (Tommy and Mike Lee leads Victor and Rico to kill The Mings)

VICTOR

For you interfering my plan, I had The Mings killed.

INT. PIER 33 - NIGHT
PRESENT TIME

KEN

Why did you kill Big Billy? Why did you shoot Laura?

VICTOR

It was the best way to call you out! After 3 years in hiding.

KEN

Where is Angie? What have you done with her?

VICTOR

Angie is alright, I plan to sell her from place to place for sex trafficking.

KEN

You do know that the Empress will kill anyone and everyone to find her daughter.

                              VICTOR
          That's the plan. War, Chaos, Anarchy and Bloodshed
          is good for business. I can turn a profit for this. A very
          large one.

Victor has his men to execute Ken

                              VICTOR
          Say hi to Maggie for me when your burning in Hell.

This enrages Liu as he draw guns -- Blowing the henchmen away.
     Victor pulls out double-barrel pistols.

HEROIC BLOODSHED SCENE:
Ken Liu leads The Suns in a gun battle with The Tongs. Johnny shoots the
Tongs. Benny snipes a few.

INT. PIER 33 (STORAGE ROOM) - CONTINUOUS
Linda and Jimmy enter the Storage Room. They are horrified to see young girls
being sold for slavery. They find Angie in a cage. They free her and other sex
trafficked victims.

                              JIMMY
          Angie.

                              ANGIE
          Jimmy.

Angie and Jimmy hug.

                              JIMMY
          We got to go.

Tiger Lady attacks. Linda makes Swiss cheese out of her.

                    LINDA
    Come on!

INT. PIER 33 - CONTINUOUS
Benny continues to snipe Tong members and Ken and Johnny kills Tong members but the numbers are great.
Victor is a more experienced and stronger gunman than Ken as he wounds him.
    Julius, Priest and Westside Syndicate arrives to join the war with the Suns.

                    JOHNNY
        Your late.

                    PRIEST
    It took a while to convince Julius.

                    JULIUS
    Where is that Victor fool?

                    KEN
        He'll be dead soon.

The Westside Syndicate GHOST SOLDIERS smokes Tongs Members. They scope every inch the building...But the terrorists and assassins...Comes out of wooden crates. Setting up a trap.

                    JOHNNY
        Crates!!! Shoot the crates!!!

The Ghost Soldiers are wiped out.
    Suddenly, Tyler Chan arrives from the ceiling, hang on a rope. Blasting Victor's men away from the crates. He sided with Ken to turn the tide.
    Tyler shows Ken how shoot-em-up is done as they wipeout the Tongs, terrorists and assassins.

KEN

You came back for the bounty?

TYLER

Yes I did. But I'm missing all the action, you don't
think I'd let you guys have all the fun.

INT. PIER 33 (WAREHOUSE) - CONTINUOUS
The Warehouse is a Maze of wooden crates. The Suns, Tyler and Ken shoot at
the crates.
    Some of them are terrorists. Some are trafficked girls ready to be shipped.

JOHNNY

Open up all crates. There are innocent kids in there.

The Suns and The Westside Syndicate opens every crate. They spared the trafficked girls and kills the terrorists.

TYLER

I've seen you shoot, Liu. Trust me, you suck. I'll show
you how it's done.

Ken reloads his guns. While, Tyler takes dead henchmen guns.

TYLER

Reload is for Pussies.

Benny uses his heat seeking googles -- scanning for assassins and traffic victims.
He Snipes straight through wooden crates killing the assassins.
    Johnny Wu is killed by Victor...Which enrages Tyler as he takes out the
Tongs and goes to his body.

TYLER

Johnny!

JOHNNY

Tyler...

TYLER

I should have listened to you.

JOHNNY

Doesn't matter. As long as your here. Friend.

TYLER

Not a friend. A Sun. We fight together, we die together.
Hang in their buddy.

JOHNNY

Take care of my wife and son...

Johnny dies. Tyler angry smokes Tongs, Terrorists and assassins.

Linda, Benny, Priest, Julius, Angie, Tyler and Ken are outnumbered. Many of the Suns and Westside Syndicate soldiers have fallen.

Then...Freddy Kim and The Dragon Boyz arrive and smokes them with their guns, turning the tide of the battle.

FREDDY KIM

Everyone follow me.

The heroes, victims all follow Freddy Kim's lead to escape.
BOOM!
An explosion occurs. Separating the Suns and Ken Liu.
Victor Mogui and Ken Liu are by themselves.

VICTOR

Just you and me, Liu.

KEN

Victor.

Victor and Ken shoot each other -- misses. Then, they have a fist fight. Both knocked out.

The FBI arrives, after a long gun battle; Ken Liu and Victor Mogui are badly wounded as they surrender to the FBI.

Briggs and Ramirez take Ken and Victor in.

AGENT BRIGGS

Ken Liu.

AGENT RAMIREZ

Don't worry, we will give you a plea bargain.

Agent Briggs pulls out an mp3 play -- a wire from Ken's suit.

AGENT RAMIREZ

Undetectable wire. Technology, Mogui.

AGENT BRIGGS

We got everything we need from Victor.

Russo and O'Neil arrives takes Ken away from Briggs and Ramirez.

AGENT RUSSO

That won't be necessary. Ken Liu and Victor Mogui you are all under arrest.

FBI rounded up all the west coast gangs. Julius is among the arrested.

AGENT BRIGGS

Sir, we got everything we need. Ken Liu, made a plea bargain.

                    AGENT O'NEIL
His plea bargain is denied.

                    AGENT RAMIREZ
You can't do that.

Agent Russo takes the mp3 player away.

                    AGENT RUSSO
You are both suspended and off this case. As for this,
we will take it to states evidence. Take him away.

Ken and Victor leave in separate Vans.

EXT. PIER 33 - CONTINUOUS
Feds are everywhere surrounding the pier. With Jimmy, Benny, Priest, Angie,
Linda, Tyler and Sammy trapped. They got nowhere to go.

                    JIMMY
Shit we're trapped.

                    SAMMY
No we're not.

A fishing boat sails towards our heroes. It's The Dragon Boyz reinforcements...
Disguised as fisherman. They Smuggled them out.

                    FREDDY KIM
Come on, guys.

The remaining heroes are surprised to see new allies.

JIMMY

Just get us to San Diego and to Las Vegas, now and fast.

FREDDY KIM

Yes, sir.

Jimmy knows something isn't right.

JIMMY

Where's Ken?

Freddy Kim rides the boat to San Diego.

JIMMY

Stop the boat. Where is Ken?

Benny and Tyler restrain him and Sammy.

BENNY

He's gone they got him. Probably dead.

SAMMY

You don't know that, he's my uncle! He knows how to handle himself.

TYLER

I'm afraid so.

Jimmy and Sammy calm down, devastated.

JIMMY

It was his idea to take them out and save my sister.

Angie listens to Jimmy's word. Confused.

SAMMY

What about my mom and Andy?

BENNY

They're safe. We sent them to Seattle.

BENNY

They are in hiding.

The heroes leave the crime scene. -- defeated.

EXT. CALIFORNIA HIGHWAY - DAY
In a twist of fate, Russo and O'Neil releases Victor and helps him escape and
heads to New York City. Russo and O'Neil turns out to be dirty FBI agents,
allowing Victor to takeover criminal empires while they'll help eradicate the
competition. San Francisco has been taken over.

AGENT RUSSO

Your free to go.

VICTOR

Thank you for taking out the competition.

AGENT O'NEIL

Hey, you paid us very well to clean up the garbage.

VICTOR

Don't thank me.

A Limo arrives -- Victor's MYSTERY PARTNER shows up, responsible for his
escape.

                            VICTOR
Everything is according to plan. Let's head to New
York to take out the competition.

                      MYSTERY PARTNER
There is one problem. The Five Families. They are
strength in numbers.

                            VICTOR
Then, we will do the same thing as we did to the Suns.
Extinction.

EXT. LAS VEGAS, NEVADA - DAY
SUPER: "Days Later"
The shining desert city of Las Vegas.

INT. LAURA'S MANSION - DAY
A Heavily Guarded Mansion, filled with Bodyguards.
    Laura watches the news.

                       AGENT RUSSO (O.S.)
Our agents and officers rounded up all the gangs of the
west coast. The War of crime is over. Peace and pros-
perity can continue now. Also, we have capture Ken
Liu. He is to be sentenced to death.

                      NEWS REPORTER (O.S.)
Sir, what about the escape of Victor Mogui? And rumors of the Empress of Crime?

                         AGENT RUSSO
Mogui is out there, we will catch him. As for the
Empress of Crime, we will gather many evidence to
prosecute her.

Laura pulls her magnum and Shoot the TV -- making a new hole.

Jimmy, Angie, Priest, Sammy, Timmy, Benny and Linda escaped with the help of Tyler and The Dragon Boyz. They retreated to Laura's Mansion.

ANGIE

Mom!

LAURA

Sweetie.

Angie hugs Laura, who is her mother.

LAURA
(to Angie)
I am glad you are safe.

(to Jimmy)
You protected my family well, Jimmy.

JIMMY

Your welcome.

The Suns, The Dragon Boyz, and the Westside Syndicate have being destroyed by The Feds, Victor Mogui, The Tongs and his army.

LAURA
I see you all made it alive, even small timers.

They watched the News of the FBI capture of Ken Liu and The Sun Clan elimination of California.

The heroes have no hope as they await their end and Victor's take over of America and eradication of gangs.

SAMMY

So what do we do now? Victor's Army just smoked the entire Underground Society in the West. Now FBI is on our ass. Why can we do something?

BENNY

Because half of our rivals and Feds against all of us here would be suicide.

LAURA

He's right. Now that our empire is gone. Ken Liu is in the cage where we have no power in there. I just got the word that he just got the death penalty.

JIMMY

Where is he?

LAURA

San Quentin.

JIMMY

Shit. He won't survive, not even a day. There is no way to get him out. Whites, Mexicans and Blacks will ice him.

Learning how to forgive and it was Ken's idea to save her, Angie wants to free Ken Liu.

ANGIE

Or can we?...Mom, you have power over the Underground Society. You and Papa use to run it.

LAURA

We did, but how can I, when we got Feds on our tails. I hate the Feds.

PRIEST

Your mother is right, it too risky. Just let him go.

LAURA

Angie, I never wanted you to be in this life.

ANGIE

No mom! You told me once to be your own person and make your own choices. And I choose to get Ken Liu out. Without you.

Laura grabs Angie's arm.

LAURA

Sorry, my dear. One criminal doesn't outweigh millions. This changes nothing.

Laura, Linda and Timmy T. objects, but Jimmy, Sammy and Benny agree.

JIMMY

It changes everything. He's not a criminal, he's my best friend. The brother I should have had. Where is your Honor, Laura? Dad would be ashamed if you let this happen. If she going to save him, so am I.

SAMMY

Count me in. He helped me a lot. He's my cousin.

TIMMY T

You guys are fucking crazy! But I'm in.

BENNY

I'm in.

LINDA

I will join but this is for the Sun Clan.

FREDDY KIM

If Sammy goes, then we go. The Dragon Boyz swears
allegiance to the underground society.

Freddy Kim goes to Laura and kisses her ring -- Out of respect. Laura grins.

LAURA

Not bad for a bunch of small-timers.

The Dragon Boyz join.
    Tyler joins in to honor his late best friend Johnny Wu, due to his experience
in jail, he can be of an assistance.

TYLER

I'll go, I know the roots of prison life in San Quentin.
Been there.

JIMMY

Same here.

JIMMY gets a phone call. Hard faced.

JIMMY

Shit. Victor is heading to NYC. My family is there.

LAURA

Then you should go to NYC to kill Victor and his
empire.

JIMMY

What about Ken, we got to save him.

LAURA

As for Ken, we'll do what we can to save him.

EXT. SAN QUENTIN COUNTY JAIL - DAY

Ken Liu is held in San Quentin where the prisoners led by Rico Blanco surround him. Ken is in solitary confinement -- Locked up like a caged animal. He is ready for them.

KEN (V.O.)

I guess this is the end of the road. No allies to back me up. Just a bunch of wolves ready to hunt... But I'll be ready for them. Something will turn up. It always does.

Ken grins...ready to fight.

To be concluded....

About the Authors

About the Authors: Born Dominic Rocky Daniels, in the city of Anaheim, California in 1984, he was raised in San Gabriel, CA. At a young age his passion has always been in films, animation, and storytelling. He is best known for his dark fantasy / vampire book series: *The Damascus Chronicles* *(Book 1)* & *The Damascus Chronicles: Denizens of the Night (Book 2)*, which has won the *Amazon Editors Choice Award: Best Books of 2014*.

Trained in fine art at the age of 10, he decided to go into the entertainment business and become a writer. He is a self-taught author and electronic dance music arranger under his Nega Blast X music production brand. He has a Bachelor Degree of Science in Media Arts and Animation from The Art Institute of California-Los Angeles. In his spare time he reads graphic novels and studies movies, his favorite music is heavy metal.

Website:

www.dominicrdaniels.com

Born as Raynaldo **De** Dios DeLeon II. **Ron** DeLeon is a fellow graduate of The Art Institute of California - Los Angeles with a Bachelor of Science degree in Video and Film Production. He is well trained in the process of professional screenwriting, crew work, video editing, and camera operation. He is best known as the Co-Creator of the ***Underground Society Series*** and his co-written thriller ***Badland.*** He has worked for Cast Iron Productions as a freelance Casting Editor on the TV show *"Blush"* for ***Lifetime Channel*** and other show projects. He worked in production at ***Fox Sports West*** in Los Angeles, CA and ***EBS Entertainment*** in Santa Monica, CA. Currently**, Ron** is a professional photographer & videographer based in Southern California. In his spare time, he shoots videos as an active video blogger and enjoys watching cult movies.

Website:

deleonpictures.tumblr.com

www.linkedin.com/in/rondeleon

https://www.facebook.com/therondeleon

www.ingramcontent.com/pod-product-compliance
Lightning Source LLC
Chambersburg PA
CBHW071240170626
46809CB00001B/25